Muffins and M... Cove Cozy Mystery Series Book 6

By Leena Clover

Copyright © Leena Clover, Author 2018

All rights reserved. No part of this publication may be reproduced, stored in a retrieval system, or transmitted, in any form, or by any means (electronic, mechanical, photocopying, recording or otherwise) without the prior written permission of the author.

This book is a work of fiction. Names, characters, places, organizations and incidents are either products of the author's imagination or used fictitiously. Any resemblance to actual events, places, organizations or persons, living or dead, is entirely coincidental.

Chapter 1

Jenny King sat out on her patio, sipping a glass of white wine. The fine mist coming off a gurgling water fountain sprayed her occasionally. The scent of wild roses and gardenias perfumed the air. The sky blazed in hues of orange and red as the sun went down over the ocean. A tea light flickered inside a hurricane lamp, teased by the brisk ocean breeze.

Jenny's aunt Star sat next to her, doodling something on her sketch pad.

"Can you see anything in this light?" Jenny asked her aunt.

"Enough," her aunt replied without looking up.

She was engrossed in her drawing. Star was a local artist who was famous for painting seascapes of the coastal Virginia region she called home. She had lived on the small barrier island of Pelican Cove for over forty five years. The seaside town was home to her. And now it was home to her niece Jenny.

Jenny had been married to a big city lawyer for twenty years. She had been a poster child for the rich suburban housewife who lunched with friends and threw parties to further her husband's career - until her husband introduced her to a younger model of herself.

Dumped and discarded at the age of forty four, Jenny had been at a crossroads. She grabbed her aunt's invitation like a lifeline and arrived in Pelican Cove. She had worked hard to build a new life for herself there.

Suddenly, Jenny swore under her breath and brandished a fly swatter in the air. She smacked a spot on the table with gusto.

"This little thing is useless," Star told her. "We should get the electric one. These mosquitoes are getting a bit too bold."

"I never thought Pelican Cove would have so many mosquitoes."

"We are at risk alright, being so close to the marshes," Star noted. "But we manage to keep these little buggers under control."

"How?"

"The town is supposed to take care of these things," Star explained. "Looks like someone dropped the ball on pest control this year."

"Look at me, talking about the mosquito population."

Jenny shook her head in wonder. Sometimes, she didn't recognize herself.

"What's wrong with that?" Star queried. "You know these bugs carry deadly diseases. They need to be handled."

"Let's go inside," Jenny said, getting up. "You can show me what you've been working on."

Star hugged her sketch book and covered it with her arms.

"It's a surprise. You can't see it yet."

"Just a peek?"

"No way, kiddo. Why don't you go up to bed and call that young man of yours?"

Jenny's face fell.

"I guess I can try."

Jenny had been dating Adam Hopkins, the local sheriff, for the past few months. Earlier in the spring, Adam had asked her to move in with him. At the time, Jenny was just getting settled in at Seaview, her newly renovated sea facing mansion. She had turned Adam down.

Her response had cooled things between the couple. They had gone on a couple of dates since then but Adam didn't drop in for dinner like he used to. Neither did he turn up for their late evening walks on the beach.

"You are both too headstrong," Star frowned. "One of you will have to take a step back."

"I'm not leaving Seaview any time soon," Jenny said. "It's my home now."

"You need to move past this cold war. I almost preferred to see you two fighting like cats and dogs."

"He just doesn't care anymore, I guess."

"Have some faith, Jenny. That boy loves you. You just need to spend more time together."

Star paused mid-step as they walked into the house.

"I know. You need a new crime to solve together. Nothing major – maybe something silly like a stolen bike or two?"

"Don't be ridiculous!" Jenny said haughtily as she climbed up the winding staircase to her room.

Jenny overslept the next morning. It was fifteen minutes past five when she pulled up in front of the Boardwalk Café. The building was dark. Jenny wondered why Petunia, the owner, had not opened the café. Usually, Petunia almost always arrived before her. Jenny was used to starting her day with a fresh cup of coffee and a warm hug from Petunia.

Jenny hurried through her routine, starting the oven. She mixed the batter for her blueberry muffins and added a generous amount of fresh blueberries. Her secret ingredient went in, the one that had people guessing.

Jenny had started working at the Boardwalk Café over a year ago at her aunt's insistence. The rest was history. Jenny's innate love for cooking had her creating tasty food every day, using the region's abundant seafood and fresh produce. People up and down the coast flocked to the café to sample her yummy treats.

Jenny pulled out the first pan of muffins and opened the café doors just as the clock chimed six. Captain Charlie, her favorite customer, came in. He was always the first one in when Jenny opened at 6 AM.

"Good morning," he greeted her, peering into the kitchen. "Do I smell muffins?"

"You do," Jenny said with a smile. "Blueberry muffins, your favorite."

"I like everything you cook," Captain Charlie said with a blush. He patted his slight paunch. "I have been overdoing the sweets ever since you got here."

Jenny placed two muffins in a brown paper bag and filled a large cup with coffee. She set them on the counter and glanced at the wall clock again. It was fifteen minutes past the hour. Jenny saw a few people come in and wondered when she would get a chance to call Petunia.

Captain Charlie must have read her mind.

"Where's Petunia?" he asked as he picked up his food. "She hasn't taken a day off in the past twenty five years."

Jenny felt a shudder run through her for a fraction of a second. She dismissed her apprehensions with a smile and a shrug.

"She'll be here soon, Captain Charlie. I'll tell her you were asking for her."

Jenny didn't get a chance to look at the clock again for the next hour or two. She baked a few more batches of muffins, brewed pot after pot of coffee and poached chicken for salad. She sighed with relief when her friend Heather walked into the café.

"Can you handle the register for me?" she asked. "I need to sit down for a minute."

Heather Morse ran the Bayview Inn with her grandmother. Her eyes clouded with concern as she watched Jenny take a deep breath.

"Have you had breakfast yet?" she asked with concern. "Why don't you grab a bite in the kitchen? I got this covered."

Jenny collapsed into a chair and broke a muffin into two. She popped half of it in her mouth and swallowed it without chewing. The clock chimed eight and Jenny remembered the call she needed to make. She dialed Petunia's number and tapped her foot impatiently as the phone rang several times before switching to voicemail.

Jenny walked out on the café's deck and stood with her hands on her hips, gazing at the Atlantic Ocean. The boardwalk stretched before her on both sides. The beach was almost deserted. She spotted a few tourists walking up from a parking lot, lugging camp chairs and coolers. They were clearly setting up for a day on the beach.

Jenny stepped closer to the edge and gave the beach another once over. A few benches were scattered across the boardwalk at regular intervals. She spotted a familiar orange scarf fluttering in the wind and shielded her eyes to get a better look. A lone figure sat on a bench, staring at the sea.

"What's she doing there?" she mumbled to herself.

Jenny climbed down the café's steps and strode across the boardwalk to the bench.

"Petunia!" she called out, raising her voice as she got closer.

The figure seated on the bench didn't budge.

Jenny stood up, wiping her tears on her sleeve.

"It's okay, girls." She looked up at Adam. "Let's go."

Adam pointed to an empty table.

"Actually, we can talk here or out on the deck, as long as we have some privacy."

Jenny shut the café doors and nodded to her aunt. The Magnolias went into the kitchen.

"Walk me through everything you did this morning," Adam ordered. "Don't leave anything out."

Jenny stared at the man who had become an important part of her life. Was she really in love with him?

She leaned forward and glared at him.

"So tell me, Adam. Are you being a jerk as usual, or are you just doing your job?"

Chapter 2

The Magnolias sat on the deck of the Boardwalk Café. The usually lively group was quiet. Jenny warmed her hands with a cup of coffee and stared at the ocean. Betty Sue's knitting needles clacked and her hands moved in a familiar rhythm as she gawked at a spot on the table. Star drew furiously in her sketch pad. Heather sat with her eyes closed and Molly held a book upside down. They were down one member and every one of them felt Petunia's absence.

"She was the kindest person I knew," Star said suddenly. "I still remember the day she took over the café."

"What did she do before that?" Jenny asked.

Star shrugged. "She came here one summer like any other tourist. I guess she fell in love with the town."

"She wasn't an islander," Betty Sue nodded. "The Boardwalk Café had been shut up for a year since the previous owner died. The next thing we know, Petunia has bought the place and is serving coffee."

"Did she have any friends other than us?" Molly asked.

"Not that I know of," Star said. "I have never seen her talking to anyone else."

"She spent most of her life here in the café," Betty Sue told them. "There wasn't a single day in the past twenty five years when she didn't open the café."

"Even for Christmas and Thanksgiving?" Jenny asked, astounded. "Didn't she celebrate it with someone?"

Star and Betty Sue shook their heads.

"She kept it open for people who had nowhere else to go."

"I miss her," Jenny said fiercely. "She gave me a chance, helped me turn my life around."

"What happens to the café now?" Heather asked.

"I'll keep running it until someone says otherwise," Jenny said. "That's the least I can do."

Jenny struggled to her feet, trying to fight off her melancholy.

"I need to start making lunch."

"I'll come and help you," her aunt offered.

"I have to get back to the library," Molly said grimly. "But call me if you need anything, Jenny."

The group dispersed and headed to their daily jobs.

Jenny chopped celery and walnuts for chicken salad.

"Unfortunately, I can't do that."

Jason pulled out a bottle of juice from a small refrigerator and handed it to Jenny.

"Have the police found anything yet?"

Jenny poured out what had happened at the police station.

"Adam's good at his job. He'll get to the bottom of this."

"When?" Jenny asked.

"You know how the law works, Jenny. You will have to be patient."

Jenny went back to the café, angrier than she had been before.

The Magnolias were sitting out on the deck again. None of them had been able to concentrate on work.

"Why don't you go out there?" her aunt suggested. "Lunch is almost ready."

"It's okay," Jenny told Star. "I'll help you dish it up."

She carried a tray loaded with chicken salad sandwiches out to the deck. Her aunt followed with a tray of drinks.

Star had taken care of the lunch rush in Jenny's absence. The Boardwalk Café was the only eating establishment of its kind in Pelican Cove. Jenny knew people depended on her for their meals. She couldn't just close the café when she needed a break.

The girls were quiet as they ate their lunch.

"Yooohooo …"

Jenny cringed as she heard a familiar greeting. A short, plump woman came up the steps from the beach. She took a seat at the table and greeted everyone.

Barb Norton was a force to reckon with in Pelican Cove. She was on various committees and was always scurrying around, working on some project or the other. The older Magnolias didn't care much for her.

"I am so sorry," Barb began. "Pelican Cove has lost a valuable member."

No one said anything.

Barb went on to talk about how Petunia had been a pillar of society.

"What do you want, Barb?" Betty Sue asked between bites of a sandwich.

"I know you were all close to Petunia," Barb said. "And I know you must be grieving. Grief can be crippling. I should know. I lost a few people close to me."

"Get to the point," Star interrupted.

"You need an outlet for your grief," Barb beamed. "And I have just the thing."

"What mad project are you taking up now?" Betty Sue asked.

"You must have noticed the mosquito menace Pelican Cove is facing. Clearly, the town has failed in their pest control efforts this year. I am forming a new committee to take care of the problem."

"What's that got to do with us?" Heather asked sharply.

"The Extermination Committee needs volunteers," Barb announced. "You need something to distract you from this sordid business. I am willing to sign you all up."

"Get out," Jenny seethed. "Just get out of here and leave us alone."

"What's the matter with her?" Barb asked the others. "You do realize I am trying to help?"

"We don't need your help," Jenny said, scrambling to her feet. "We will grieve for Petunia as long as we want and any way we want. How dare you come up here and talk about some useless committee."

Barb puffed up with indignation.

"Useless? The Extermination Committee is not useless. Do you know how deadly mosquitoes can be? We are facing a possible outbreak of West Nile or Zika in Pelican Cove."

"That's fine," Star said. "But you need to leave now, Barb."

"I'm just trying to help!"

"But you're not helping," Betty Sue roared. "Go peddle your project somewhere else."

Barb Norton turned red and stomped down the café steps.

"Unbelievable," Molly fumed. "That woman is vile!"

"She's not entirely wrong," Betty Sue said.

She looked at Jenny.

"I know you have your hands full with the café. But you can't just sit around crying over what happened."

"What do you want me to do, Betty Sue?"

"Find out who killed Petunia."

"She's right, Jenny," Star said. "You have done it before. Use your skills to get to the bottom of this. It's the only way we can get justice for our friend."

"Petunia was shot with a gun," Jenny reminded them. "I have no idea why anyone would do that."

"That's exactly what we need to find out," Heather said. "I'll be your wing woman. In fact, we will all pitch in and help."

"Star and I can take care of the café," Betty Sue agreed. "You girls get busy talking to people."

"Adam won't like it."

"Since when have you done what Adam wanted?" Molly asked.

"Don't let him rule your life, Jenny," Heather added.

"We are not detectives," Jenny reasoned.

"This won't be the first time you solved a murder, Jenny," Star said grimly. "What's holding you back?"

"My friend wasn't the victim all those times," Jenny said, as a tear rolled down her cheek. "I can't be objective about this."

"That's fine," Star said. "Because this is as personal as it gets."

"She's right!" Molly and Heather chorused. "We need you on board, Jenny."

Jenny thought of the sweet old woman who had been a guiding force in her life for the past year and a half. She was just beginning to get to know her. Jenny took a deep breath as her heart filled with a new resolve. She was going to do whatever it took to catch Petunia's killer.

"Let's do this," she said, putting her hand on Heather's. Molly joined in, followed by Star and Betty Sue.

Jenny's eyes burned as she looked around at her friends.

"Best of luck to us."

Chapter 3

Jenny tried to run the Boardwalk Café by herself. She had known Petunia silently did a giant's share of work at the café. She didn't mind the extra work. But she hadn't realized how much she relied on Petunia for the little things. She found herself turning around to ask questions – how many batches of muffins to bake, how much flour to order – only to find out that she was on her own now. Petunia wasn't going to offer any advice in her soft voice.

The Magnolias clung to their routine with a tacit agreement. Betty Sue arrived at 10 AM every morning, lugging her knitting, with Heather close behind. Star and Molly completed the circle.

"Who would you say knew Petunia the best?" Jenny asked one day as they sat out on the deck.

September had brought cool breezes to Pelican Cove but it was still warm enough to sit outside without a jacket or sweater.

"She was a quiet one," Star said. "We knew her well, Betty Sue and I. We have been meeting here every morning forever."

"Even before I came back to town?" Heather asked.

Heather had been away at college and then she had worked in the city for a few years. She had come back to Pelican Cove in her late twenties.

Star nodded.

"You and Molly were in the city. My Jenny wasn't here either."

"She never talked about where she came from?" Jenny asked, surprised.

"She was from somewhere up north," Betty Sue said. "I think she was a widow."

"You think?" Heather pressed. "You don't know for sure?"

"Petunia wasn't very forthcoming about her past life," Star explained. "We realized that early on. We didn't want to pester her about it."

"You think she didn't talk about it for a reason?" Jenny mused.

"I always thought something painful had happened to her," Betty Sue said sagely. "Clearly, she didn't want to relive her past. And I didn't think it was my place to remind her of it."

"I get what you're saying …" Jenny began. "But she never volunteered anything in all these years?"

Star and Betty Sue shook their heads sadly.

"Now we will never know, I suppose," Betty Sue added.

The talk turned to finding out who had murdered Petunia.

"Have you thought of how you are going to begin your search?" Molly asked Jenny.

"Well, I start with people close to the victim. In this case, that's us. I try to learn about any recent events in the victim's life, ask if the victim had any enemies."

She looked around at her friends.

"Can you think of anything out of the ordinary that might have happened this week?"

"Why was Petunia on the beach that morning?" Betty Sue asked immediately.

"And what was she doing there?" Star added. "Shouldn't she have been here at the café, helping you with the morning crowd?"

"Petunia liked to watch the sun rise over the ocean," Jenny told them. "She lingered on the beach sometimes before coming in. But she was always here before me."

"What time was that?" Molly asked, pulling out a notebook and scribbling in it.

Jenny was glad Molly was taking notes. She was too distracted to keep all the facts straight in her head.

"Well, she was here around 5 every day, or earlier. She came in before me and opened the café."

"So when did she watch the sunrise?" Heather asked. "Did she go out during the breakfast rush?"

"She would step outside sometimes," Jenny shrugged.

"She didn't come in at all on that day, right?" Betty Sue asked. "Do you mean to say she had been on the beach all along?"

"We don't know the time of her death," Jenny reminded them. "That's something the police will have to tell us. And it's anybody's guess when that will happen."

"Have you talked to Adam?" Molly asked.

"Not since that day," Jenny said, shaking her head. "He can call me whenever he wants."

"You know how Adam is about his job," Heather said. "Don't let it come between you, Jenny."

"Says you?" Jenny asked, rolling her eyes. "Since when

did you start giving relationship advice, Heather?"

"Since I learned a bitter lesson or two," Heather shot back. "Ego has no place in love."

"If Adam loves me, he has a weird way of showing it."

"Can you be sure Petunia never came in that day?" Betty Sue asked, setting her knitting aside.

Jenny thought back for a minute.

"I didn't use my key, so the café wasn't locked. She must have come in for a few minutes, I guess."

"So she opened the door for you and then went on the beach right away? Did she do that a lot?"

"Never," Jenny told them. "Petunia brewed the first batch of coffee before I got here. And she used to prep everything for me and turn the oven on."

Jenny held up a hand when she saw her aunt lean forward to ask the next question.

"None of it was done that day. I made the coffee myself."

"I'm writing this down as an outstanding question," Molly remarked. "Why did Petunia go out that morning?"

The group broke up soon after that. Jenny had to get ready for the lunch rush. She chopped vegetables and added them to a big stock pot for making soup.

Her aunt mixed the crab salad.

"You should be at the gallery, or out on a beach somewhere, working on your art," Jenny told her.

"Hush, Jenny," her aunt said. "I am exactly where I need to be."

"How long am I going to impose on you?" Jenny asked. "I have to learn to handle everything by myself."

"Give yourself some time," Star said. "Have you thought of hiring some permanent help?"

Jenny and Petunia hired some students to help them with the summer rush. The kids were back in school.

"I haven't considered that yet," Jenny admitted. "I feel it's too soon."

"You can never replace Petunia," Star read her mind. "We all know that."

Jenny stirred the pot of soup and stared at the wall, lost in thought.

"I need to order supplies for the week ahead," she

sighed.

Star pointed to a drawer.

"Petunia was a meticulous record keeper. You should find all her lists in there."

Jenny rifled through the drawer and pulled out a small notebook titled Supplies.

"It's all in here," she nodded.

Petunia had kept copious notes about what needed to be done every week of the month. There was a list of wholesalers she worked with at the back of the book with a rating for each of them.

"There's a treasure trove of information here," Jenny marveled as she pulled out more stuff from the drawer.

Her eyes fell on an appointment book.

"What's this?" she muttered.

It was a small diary with a blue leather cover. Jenny hesitated a bit before opening it.

"Have you seen this before?" Jenny asked her aunt, waving the blue colored book at her. "It looks like a planner of sorts, or an appointment diary. There's a note for a doctor's appointment here, for example. And a dentist's appointment."

"You know we don't use phones or computers to write down our appointments," Star said. "It's how we keep track of the calendar the old fashioned way."

Jenny flipped the pages furiously, searching for something.

"Did I say anything wrong?" Star asked her.

"Not at all. You just gave me a big clue."

Jenny pulled up a page and jabbed her finger at what was written down there.

She sat down next to her aunt and showed her what she had found.

"5 A. M, P/W," she said out loud. "So Petunia was planning to meet someone on the beach that day."

"At 5 in the morning?" Star asked, raising her eyebrows in disbelief.

"Give me a few minutes," Jenny said.

She flipped through the diary again, going slow this time.

"She has this appointment listed on the same day of every month," Jenny said triumphantly. "Who is this 'P/W'? Can you think of anyone?"

"I'm still trying to wrap my head around this," Star muttered. "Why meet someone at 5 in the morning?"

"I need to think about this," Jenny said.

She went out on the deck and began pacing. If Petunia had kept her appointment, she must have been at the bench by 5 AM. That meant she had been killed any time between 5 and 8.

Jenny looked up and saw a familiar figure sitting in the sand. He wore tattered clothes that had clearly seen better days. His salt and pepper beard was as dirty as his face. Jenny had been surprised to see a homeless person in Pelican Cove. The man turned up on the beach sometime in the morning and walked around all day. She would find him writing something in the sand with a stick, then wiping it off with his foot. He did that over and over again. Jenny had wondered if she should offer him anything to eat.

The man turned around and stared directly at the café. Jenny tried to ward off a sudden nervous feeling.

"Hello there," she called out. "How's it going?"

The man shrugged and looked away.

A group of people walked up to the café and Jenny went in. It was time for the lunch rush.

Star was sitting at the kitchen table, looking smug.

There was a pile of blue colored notebooks in front of her.

"Look what I found in that drawer."

"Old diaries?" Jenny asked listlessly.

"Old appointment books," her aunt corrected her. "These go back five years. And all of them list the same appointment."

Jenny's eyes gleamed with interest.

"You mean Petunia was meeting someone early in the morning for the past five years?"

"At least that," her aunt nodded.

"She must have trusted this person," Jenny said thoughtfully. "You think he or she is the one who shot her?"

Star shrugged.

"We need to find this person," she said. "Only they can tell us what happened that day."

"But how do we find this 'P/W'?" Jenny asked, sounding defeated.

Jenny got busy filling lunch orders with her aunt's help. The two ladies finally sat back in the kitchen to eat their own lunch.

"Ready to call it a day?" Star asked.

"Why don't you take the car?" Jenny said. "I need to stretch my legs a bit. I will go to the seafood market on my way back."

Jenny checked the next day's menu and prepped as much as she could. She closed the café and walked to Williams Seafood Market. Her friend and Molly's fiancé Chris Williams greeted her.

"How are you holding up, Jenny?" he asked kindly.

Jenny shrugged, swallowing a lump in her throat. She had plodded through the day somehow but it was all coming back to her.

"I'll have the usual, please," she told Chris.

Chris packed a pound of shrimp and three fillets of the catch of the day.

"The catch just came in," he assured her.

Jenny took the package without a word and started walking back home.

A stream of big black SUVs suddenly passed her, stirring up a cloud of dust. Jenny stopped in her tracks, thrown aback by the onslaught. The car windows were so dark it was impossible to see inside. The lead car screeched to a stop with a spin of its tires. The other cars followed suit.

A man jumped out of the car at the front and summoned Jenny.

He was tall and wide and his gigantic belly wobbled every time he moved. He wore a dark shirt and trousers and a black leather jacket. He held out a small piece of paper and asked Jenny for directions.

"What's the holdup, Six Pac?" a high pitched voice demanded from inside.

"Just a minute, Boss!" the man yelled, snatching the paper from Jenny's hands.

"Thanks, doll," he crooned as he climbed back into the car and slammed the door.

The tires spun again and the cars sped off, leaving Jenny standing in the middle of the road, her mouth hanging open.

Chapter 4

Jenny began her day at the Boardwalk Café the next morning.

She chopped sweet peppers for her crab omelet. It was the most popular breakfast special at the Boardwalk Café. She tore off some fresh dill from a bunch and ran her knife through it.

She heard someone come into the café and went outside to take their order. Adam Hopkins stood in his uniform, his hands behind his back.

"Morning, Jenny," he greeted her. "How about a spot of breakfast?"

"Why not?" Jenny said sweetly. "This is a café, after all."

She pulled out a pad and pencil from her apron pocket and asked Adam for his order.

"I'll have whatever you are cooking," he grinned.

Jenny refused to smile back.

She went in and started cooking the omelets. She toasted some whole grain bread while the eggs cooked and put everything on a tray. She added small pots of butter and preserves. She placed the tray before Adam with a bang.

"Thank you," Adam said, picking up his knife and fork.

Heavy footsteps sounded outside. A group of men came in with much fanfare. Jenny assumed they were tourists.

A brown haired man of medium height strode into the café. He wore a three piece suit the color of butter cream. A fedora sat on his head and a cigar dangled from his lips. He was flanked by three men, all wearing neatly pressed shirts and trousers and leather jackets. Jenny recognized the man who had asked her for directions.

"There's no smoking in here," she said.

"Relax, sweetheart," the guy wearing the hat said. "It's not lit."

His high pitched voice grated on Jenny's nerves.

"Can I get you a table?" she asked.

The man in the hat held out his hand.

"Vincenzo Bellini," he offered. "Call me Vinny."

"Hello," Jenny nodded.

She was feeling mystified.

"I'm here to talk about my Ma."

"I'm sorry, but I don't know your mother."

"Sure you do," Vinny said. "She owned this café, didn't she?"

"What nonsense!" Jenny exclaimed.

The three men flanking Vinny sprung into action. Jenny found herself surrounded by them all of a sudden.

"Hey, hey, take it easy, boys," Vinny drawled. "We're just talking here."

"My Ma ran this café for twenty five years," Vinny spoke up. "I'm here to take her home."

Jenny sat down with a thud.

"Are you talking about Petunia?"

Vinny nodded.

"That's the name she went by here. But her real name was Leona."

"I didn't know Petunia had a son," Jenny explained. "She, err, didn't mention she had any kids."

"She had two boys," Vinny said in a matter of fact voice. "The other one lives in California."

Adam stood up and cleared his throat. Jenny had forgotten all about him.

"See you later, Jenny," he said meaningfully and walked out of the café.

Jenny turned back to the man called Vinny.

"How can I help you?"

"I don't need your help, sweetheart. I'm just here to take my Ma home."

"How about some breakfast, doll?" one of Vinny's posse spoke up.

Jenny finally looked at him and tried not to wince. He had a scar on his face, extending from his mouth in a line parallel to his eyes. It looked like a sneer.

Vinny let out a string of expletives.

"Smiley here's been hungry all morning. You think you can feed him something?"

"Sure," Jenny stammered. "How about a blueberry muffin?"

Jenny brought out a basket of muffins and poured

fresh coffee. She made omelets for the lot. She had spotted a gun poking out from Smiley's jacket when she poured the coffee. Her hands shook when she placed the platters of food before them.

"Relax, doll," the man called Six Pac said. "We are not here to hurt you."

"Unless you whacked my Ma," Vinny laughed.

"Of course I didn't," Jenny bristled.

The men finished their food and stood up to leave. Vinny put a 100 dollar bill on the table.

"We'll be in touch," he nodded.

Jenny heard tires squealing outside and guessed the men had left in their big black cars. She pulled her apron off and almost jogged to the police station.

Adam was standing in the lobby, reading a file.

"Let's go in," he said, ushering her into his office.

"What's going on?" Jenny asked him, her hands on her hips. "Who were those men?"

Adam leaned back in his chair and put his arms behind his head.

"The mob has arrived in Pelican Cove, Jenny."

"What are you talking about?" Jenny asked, puzzled.

"Vinny 'Twix' Bellini is the scion of the infamous Bellini family."

"Infamous for what?"

"They are a mob family from New Jersey," Adam said coolly. "Enzo Bellini is the head of the family. They call him the Hawk. He's over 85 but he still calls the shots."

"What are they doing here?"

"Didn't you hear what Vinny said?" Adam asked her. "Petunia was his mother."

"You really believe that?"

"I have been reading up on them since last night," Adam sighed. "State authorities notified us as soon as the Bellinis entered Virginia. Petunia Clark was actually Leona Bellini, Enzo's daughter and Vinny's mother."

"Are you saying Petunia was a criminal?"

Adam shook his head.

"There is no record of that. Petunia just came from a crime family. I am guessing she wanted to escape from it."

"You're saying she came to Pelican Cove to get away?"

"Looks like it."

"Why are they here? What am I supposed to do?"

"They are her next of kin," Adam said reluctantly. "I suppose they are really here to take her back."

"How can they roam around freely if they are criminals?"

"The Bellinis went legit long ago," Adam explained. "They have a string of different businesses – laundries, pizzerias, meat shops – you name it."

"They are carrying guns, Adam," Jenny burst out. "I saw a gun poking out from one guy's jacket."

"He probably has a permit for it."

"Is that all you are going to say?"

"Look. I don't think they are here to make trouble. They will be gone before you know it."

"I hope you're right, Sheriff," Jenny muttered and walked out.

She crossed the road and knocked on Jason's door.

"Jenny!" Jason greeted her with a smile. "I was just about to call you."

"Do you know what's going on in town?" Jenny asked, her chest heaving.

"The Bellinis are here," Jason said calmly.

"You knew?" Jenny exclaimed. "It's all true, then."

"I'm afraid so," Jason said with pursed lips.

"Did we know Petunia at all?" Jenny wailed. "Wait, that wasn't even her real name."

"You need to calm down, Jenny," Jason soothed. "Whatever her name, she was your friend."

"Was she?"

Jason opened a file in front of him.

"The Magnolias meant a lot to her. She left specific instructions for you regarding her last wishes."

"I don't think Vinny's going to like that."

"He doesn't have a choice in the matter," Jason said.

"How long have you been her lawyer, Jason?" Jenny asked.

"For a while. Why?"

"Who else did she hang out with other than us?"

"Honestly, the only people I have seen Petunia talking to were your aunt and Betty Sue. And the people who came into the café, of course."

Jenny told him about the man Petunia had supposedly met every month.

"That's news to me," Jason admitted. "Sounds a bit hush-hush, meeting someone at five in the morning."

"Looks like she was a pro at hiding stuff," Jenny said bitterly.

Petunia had deceived them all and Jenny wasn't happy about it.

"Don't be too hard on her, Jenny," Jason sighed. "Maybe she didn't have a choice."

Jenny returned to the café with a heavy heart. There was a mad rush at the café for lunch and Jenny barely had a minute to spare. Vinny and his posse came back for lunch. Jenny knew they had very few choices to eat out in Pelican Cove. That meant they were living somewhere in town.

Jenny talked to Captain Charlie later that day.

"I'm trying to make a list of Petunia's friends. Did you see her talking to someone in particular?"

"Your aunt and Betty Sue were about the only friends

she had," Captain Charlie said. "And you young girls, of course."

"She must have had other friends in town?" Jenny persisted.

"I don't think so," Captain Charlie said. "Say. What's this I hear about some thugs claiming they knew our Petunia?"

"It's true."

Jenny gave Captain Charlie the short version. He whistled in amazement.

Jenny went to the café early the next morning. She made coffee and put a batch of muffins into the oven. Then she took a photo of Petunia and went out on the beach.

A few runners appeared at one end. Jenny stopped them and showed them the photo.

"Did you see this woman talking to anyone on this beach?"

Her first few attempts were futile. A woman walking a golden retriever seemed eager to chat.

"Everyone knew Petunia. It's a shame what happened to her."

"Do you come here often?" Jenny asked.

"Every morning, come rain or shine," the woman boasted. "This guy won't let me sleep," she said, ruffling her dog's coat. "We usually hit the beach by 5:30. Sometimes even before that."

"Have you ever seen Petunia walking around?"

"Sometimes," the woman nodded. "She used to sit on a bench, watching the sun come up."

"Did you see her talking to anyone?"

"We chatted sometimes," the woman nodded. "That is, when she wasn't hanging out with that friend."

Jenny tried to curb her excitement.

"Is he local?"

"I guess," the woman shrugged. "Must be, right? I've seen him here plenty of times."

Jenny thanked the woman and hurried back to her café. She was sure the mysterious 'P/W' did exist. Now she just needed to find out who he was.

Jenny served a few people and put a fresh batch of muffins in the oven. She stepped out on the beach again, armed with Petunia's photo.

Her queries yielded some more information this time. She could barely wait for the Magnolias.

The women were seated on the deck, sipping their mid-morning coffee.

"Guess what I found," Jenny said, her eyes shining. "I'm sure 'P/W' is a guy. Tall, dark, probably a local."

"That doesn't tell us much," Molly complained. "Could you be more specific?"

"That's all I found out," Jenny said glumly.

"Who's that?" Heather said suddenly.

She had spotted Vinny and his posse on the beach. Vinny was walking a beagle, dressed in a suit and his signature hat. The leather jackets tagged along behind him.

"Aren't they staying at the Bayview Inn?" Jenny asked.

Vinny looked up just then and waved. He came up the steps to talk to the women. Six Pac took the leash from him and scooped up the beagle in his arms.

"Howdy ladies," he greeted them. "That lawyer fella told me what my Ma wanted. I'm cool with it."

Star looked at him with interest. Betty Sue had dropped her knitting and was muttering something under her breath.

"Do you know someone called 'P/W'?" Jenny asked suddenly.

"What kinda name is that?" Vinny asked. "Never heard of him."

"Looks like your mother knew him or her."

"My Ma walked out on me when I was 17. I never saw her after that. She might have known Spiderman for all I know."

"I'm sorry," Jenny said.

"It's not your fault, sweetheart."

Vinny turned around and walked down the steps. Jenny saw him take the beagle in his arms and hug it as he walked away.

Why had Petunia deserted her family? Did it have any bearing on why someone shot her?

Chapter 5

The rays of the setting sun bathed the garden at Seaview in a golden glow. In her newly renovated kitchen, Jenny tore basil leaves and added them to the pasta salad. The fish had been pan fried in a lemon butter sauce. Star's favorite shrimp had been tossed in the same butter and sprinkled with Old Bay seasoning. It was the signature spice of the island. No meal was complete without it.

"Dinner's ready," she called out.

Star and Jimmy Parsons walked into the dining room, hand in hand. Jimmy had been better known as the town drunk for several years. His family owned the Pelican Cove light house and a small piece of land attached to it. Jenny had discovered Jimmy's feelings for her aunt. He had cleaned up his act and had been sober for a while. Star reciprocated his feelings and the two had become inseparable.

"This salad is delicious, Jenny," Jimmy complimented her.

They were halfway through the meal when Jimmy asked Jenny about Petunia.

"Any luck?"

Jenny shook her head.

"Did you know Petunia had family in New Jersey? Apparently, they are a different kind of family."

"They are living in one of my cottages," Jimmy disclosed.

Star looked at him in surprise.

"You never told me that."

"I didn't know myself," Jimmy admitted. "Some girl called me claiming to be assistant to the head of a company. Said he wanted to spend some time on the Shore. I had no idea who was going to turn up."

"So that's where Vinny is staying," Jenny muttered.

"Him and his posse," Jimmy nodded. "They paid up for two months in advance."

"Two months? What are they going to do here for that long?"

"No idea."

"Do you think this man Petunia met secretly might have been Vinny?" Jenny asked her aunt.

"What man?" Jimmy asked, cutting a big chunk of his fish.

Jenny told him about the entries in Petunia's diary.

"Someone on the beach must have seen them."

"I asked a lot of people," Jenny explained. "All I know is he's some tall, dark guy. That could be anyone."

"Don't forget 'P/W'," her aunt reminded her.

"What's that?"

"That's how Petunia referred to the meeting in her diary," Jenny told Jimmy. "We have no idea what they mean."

"They could be initials of the person," Jimmy said.

"I never thought of that!" Jenny exclaimed. "Where's the phone book? Maybe this person is listed in it."

"Shouldn't take long," Star said. "How many people have a name starting with W anyway?"

Jimmy had cleaned his plate. He pushed it away and sipped his lemonade.

"Wait a minute. I know a 'P/W'."

"What?" Star and Jenny cried together.

"Peter Wilson," he said flatly. "You know him well, Star."

"The auto shop guy?" Star scoffed. "Why would Petunia go and meet him at 5 in the morning?"

"The initials match," Jimmy reminded her.

"Who is this guy?" Jenny asked.

"Car mechanic," Jimmy said, draining his lemonade. "Has an auto shop in town – Wilson Auto Shop? You must have seen it, Jenny. It's about a quarter mile on your left when you drive off the bridge and enter Pelican Cove."

Jenny had never noticed the auto shop.

"Petunia hid a lot from us," Jenny reminded her aunt. "Who knows what business she had with this Wilson guy?"

"Only one way to find out," Jimmy said.

Jenny was at the Boardwalk Café at 5 AM the next morning. Star arrived a couple of hours later to help her.

Jason Stone walked in after the breakfast rush had abated.

"Just the man I wanted to see," Jenny squealed.

Jason gave her a dubious smile. "What's going on, Jenny?"

"Do you know a Peter Wilson?"

"The car mechanic? Sure. Almost everyone in town knows him."

"Can you go with me to meet him?"

"Your car acting up? Why don't I take a look at it?"

Jenny shook her head.

"My car's fine. I'll bring you up to speed on the way."

Jenny packed a chocolate muffin for Jason's breakfast and handed him a large cup of coffee. She promised her aunt she would be back before the lunch rush. Grabbing another muffin for herself, she propelled Jason out of the café.

Jason munched on his muffin while Jenny explained who Peter Wilson was.

"You think he's going to be upfront with you?" he quizzed.

Jenny didn't have an answer for that.

Peter Wilson was a tall, dark haired man dressed in grease stained jeans and flannel. Jenny guessed he was a few years older than her.

He gave Jenny a curious look and shook hands with

Jason.

"Something wrong with that fancy car of yours?" he asked.

"Jenny here wants to talk to you about something."

"Hi," Jenny began. "My name is Jenny King. I work at the Boardwalk Café with Petunia."

"I know who you are," Peter Wilson nodded. "My wife loves your cupcakes. They are something else."

Jenny thanked him for the compliment.

"Do you know Petunia Clark?" she asked tentatively. "I mean, did you know her?"

"Sure," Peter Wilson shrugged. "Everyone in town knew her."

"Did you know her personally?"

Peter Wilson wiped a wrench with a dirty rag.

"What are you getting at?"

"Look. You know someone shot Petunia, right?" Jenny's voice quavered a bit but she plunged ahead. "I'm trying to find out what happened."

Peter's eyebrows shot up.

"You think I had something to do with it?"

"I found an appointment book," Jenny explained. "It says Petunia was going to meet you that day at 5 AM."

Jenny crossed her fingers behind her back while she spoke.

Peter's face crumpled.

"I was supposed to meet her, okay? But I didn't. My kid was sick. I was in the emergency room all night with my wife. That's where I heard about what happened."

"What was your meeting about?"

"It was private business," Peter Wilson shrugged again. "You don't need to know."

"Petunia's gone now," Jenny reasoned. "Look, I'm not sure how you knew her. But it looks like you had been meeting her for a while. Don't you want her killer found?"

Peter Wilson hesitated.

"I was just keeping an eye on her," he finally said. "Making sure she was alright."

"Why would you do that?"

"It's a long story," Peter said grudgingly. "I knew her way back when."

Jenny's eyes widened.

"Did you know her as Leona?"

Peter Wilson finally showed some emotion.

"Where did you get that name?"

"Vinny told me everything," Jenny said smugly. "Vinny Bellini. He was Petunia's son."

"Vinny's in town," Jason added. "Do you know him?"

"Vinny doesn't know about me, okay?" Peter Wilson burst out. "I work for the Hawk."

"Your secret's safe with us," Jenny assured him. "Why don't you tell us everything?"

"Leona, she walked out on the family one day. The Hawk, that's her papa, told me to keep an eye on her. I followed her down the coast to this little town. I been here ever since."

"So you're with the family?" Jenny asked.

Peter Wilson shrugged.

"I was twenty five when I came here. I set up this garage and stayed on. I met a local girl and married her.

59

I never went back."

"Why were you meeting Petunia?"

"We have been meeting once a month for twenty five years," Peter said. "My job was to make sure she was doing okay. I called the Hawk and let him know how his little girl was doing."

"Petunia knew that?"

Peter shrugged.

"It was the only way the Hawk would let her live on her own."

"Why meet at 5 in the morning?"

"It was her idea." Peter shrugged again.

"Do you have any idea who shot her?" Jenny asked.

"Leona's secret was safe here. People forgot about her a long time ago."

Jenny and Jason drove back to town.

"Do you think he's a mobster too?" Jenny asked him.

"Ask your boyfriend," Jason grinned. "You should tell him about Peter."

They went to the police station and walked into

Adam's office. Adam thanked them for the information.

"So Peter Wilson is part of the Bellini family? That's news to us."

"Any other updates?" she asked Adam.

"We are doing our job," Adam told her curtly.

"What now?" Jenny said when they came out of the police station.

Barb Norton waved at her from a sidewalk. She seemed to have forgotten about their earlier altercation.

"What is she up to now?" Jenny muttered to Jason.

"Do you have a few minutes, Jenny?" Jason asked. "We need to discuss something."

They went to Jason's office.

"What is it?" Jenny asked urgently.

"It's about Petunia's will," Jason admitted. "Can we talk about it now?"

"Is this about her last wishes? Maybe we should get all the Magnolias here."

"It's more than that," Jason hastened to explain. "This

particularly concerns you."

"How so?"

"She left you the Boardwalk Café."

"I plan to continue working there," Jenny assured him. "As long as I'm not booted out."

"That's just it, Jenny," Jason smiled. "You own it free and clear. It's yours to do with as you please. Petunia hoped you would continue running it though."

"What?" Jenny cried. "I don't believe it. Why would she do that? She barely knew me."

"You meant a lot to her, Jenny. The rest of her estate will be settled between her sons."

"She had more money?" Jenny asked, surprised.

"Millions," Jason nodded. "It was part of her big inheritance from her father. She never touched it. Vinny and his brother get it all."

"I need a drink," Jenny said, still feeling dazed. "What am I going to do with the café, Jason?"

"Just keep working your magic," Jason laughed. "And keep supplying me with chocolate cake."

Jason pulled out a chilled bottle of water from the

refrigerator and handed it to Jenny.

"I would much rather have her by my side," Jenny said softly.

"I know," Jason said, squeezing her trembling hand.

The midmorning sun warmed her back as Jenny walked back to the café, feeling guilty about benefiting from her friend's death. She thought about selling the café and donating the money to charity. But she loved the Boardwalk Café. She could picture herself working there for years, baking sweet treats, making chocolates and feeding locals and tourists healthy, wholesome meals.

Jenny struggled with her thoughts as she fried shrimp for the lunch special. She generously sprinkled them with seasoning and assembled the po' boy sandwiches that were so popular. She put two sandwiches in a brown paper bag and went out on the deck. Her eyes scanned the beach, searching for a familiar figure.

The man stood at the water's edge, drawing something in the sand with his stick.

"Hello there," Jenny called out, walking toward him.

The man stared at her through hooded eyes.

Jenny offered him the brown paper bag.

"I am trying out a new recipe. Why don't you tell me how you like it?"

"I don't take charity," the man mumbled.

"It's not charity," Jenny said hastily. "You'd be doing me a favor. I really need some feedback."

The man peered into the bag suspiciously. He pulled out the roll, bursting with crunchy fried shrimp. He stared at it longingly.

"Please," Jenny said. "I need your help."

The man took a small bite and chewed slowly. He took a bigger bite and wolfed the sandwich down in two minutes.

"It's good," he said. "A bit spicy."

"I'll tone down the spice then," Jenny agreed.

The man was pulling out the second sandwich.

"Are you from around here?" she asked. "I'm new in town myself."

"Came here for a job," the man offered reluctantly.

"Me too," Jenny said. "Where's your family?"

"Up in the mountains," the man mumbled.

"My son lives away from me too," Jenny volunteered. "I miss him."

The man laughed suddenly. He had finished eating the sandwich. He thrust the brown paper bag in Jenny's hands. He picked up his stick and gave her a salute.

Before Jenny could say anything else, the man turned his back on her and started walking away. He scratched something in the sand with his stick and rubbed it off with his foot, muttering to himself.

Jenny realized she didn't even know his name.

Chapter 6

The Magnolias had gathered on the deck of the Boardwalk Café.

"We need to send our girl off in style," Betty Sue ordained. "Spare no effort or expense."

"Petunia left clear instructions about what she wants," Star reminded her.

"We'll do all that," Jenny nodded. "And we'll throw her the biggest party this town has ever seen. Right here at the Boardwalk Café."

"That's a great idea, Jenny," Molly said eagerly. "How can I help?"

"We'll have a party alright," Heather said emphatically. "But what about finding out who shot Petunia? Have you made any progress at all, Jenny?"

Jenny told them about meeting Peter Wilson.

"Adam says his real name is Fabio Lombardi. He was being trained as a capo or something before he dropped everything and came here."

"So he gave up a fancy career in the mob to come look after our Petunia?" Heather asked.

"Sounds like it," Jenny agreed.

"Does he have a gun?" Molly asked. "Why couldn't he be our shooter?"

"He was more like a bodyguard, remember?" Jenny said. "And he has an alibi. He was in the hospital all night, taking care of his sick kid."

"Bummer," Heather said. "That would have been too easy."

"Does anyone benefit from Petunia's death?" Betty Sue asked. "Isn't that what you always look for, Jenny?"

"You're right, Betty Sue. Jason told me Petunia left all her money to her sons."

"So that goon Vinny benefits?" Molly asked.

"He's not going to kill his mother for a few dollars," Star dismissed.

"She walked away from him," Jenny mused. "And it's not just a few dollars, Star. Jason said it's in millions."

"Maybe you should talk to him," Betty Sue said grimly.

Heather and Molly jumped up.

"We are coming with you, Jenny."

"He's living in one of Jimmy's cottages," Jenny said. "It's barely a mile out."

Jenny told them to settle down. She assembled some sandwiches for lunch and made sure Star could handle the crowd by herself.

Vinny walked into the café just as they were getting ready to leave.

"Hello sweetheart," he said, smiling at Jenny.

Vinny was dressed in another cream colored suit, with his signature hat perched jauntily on his head. His three companions wore their uniform of dark clothes and leather jackets. Jenny figured they spent more on their wardrobe than she did.

"I was just coming to see you, Vinny," Jenny said.

"It's my lucky day," he smiled. "How about a spot of lunch? We are starving."

Jenny led them out on the deck.

"I would kill for this view," Vinny drawled.

He laughed heartily when he saw the expression on Jenny's face.

"Relax, I'm joking."

Six Pac, Smiley and the third man sprawled on the chairs around Vinny. Jenny had learned he was called Biggie. He was barely five feet tall and weighed under a hundred pounds.

Chowder was on the menu that day, with tomato mozzarella sandwiches. Vinny tucked a napkin under his chin and started on his soup. He waved a hand at Jenny.

"What did you want to talk about?"

"Jason told me Petunia left you a lot of money."

Vinny shrugged.

"A little bit. Why?"

"How do I know you didn't shoot her for the money?"

Vinny put the spoon back in his soup. His eyes had turned hard.

"You think I killed my Ma?"

"You could have," Jenny said boldly. "Where were you that day between 5 and 8."

"I was up in Jersey sleeping next to my wife," Vinny said coldly. "Not that I owe you any explanation."

Smiley spoke up.

"You got some guts, lady."

"A few million dollars is a lot of money," Jenny mumbled.

"You know how much money I got?" Vinny asked her with a smile. "I have billions, in this country and offshore. I don't need the money."

"Maybe you had a grudge against her," Jenny shrugged.

"For the last time, lady, I didn't whack my Ma."

Vinny slurped the last of his soup and picked up his sandwich.

"Someone told me you are some hotshot detective. Is this all you got?"

"Money is generally a big motive," Jenny persisted.

"That lawyer told me my Ma left you this café," Vinny said. "How do I know you didn't pull the trigger?"

"I would never do that!" Jenny said, sucking in her breath. "I loved Petunia. She gave me a chance when I had nothing."

"Okay," Vinny said, nodding his head. "So you and I both had nothing to do with it. Let's agree on that, shall we?"

Jenny found herself nodding her head.

"I want you to find out who shot my Ma," Vinny continued. "Name your price."

"I don't want money," Jenny said, scandalized. "I want justice for Petunia."

"Okay then," Vinny said. "Just let me know if I can help."

Vinny and his goons stayed on the deck for the next couple of hours, eating pie and drinking coffee.

Jenny walked to the police station as soon as they left.

"Any updates?" she asked Adam. "Do you have any suspects yet?"

"One or two," Adam said, looking at her thoughtfully.

"Who is it?" Jenny asked. "Her sons inherit millions from her death. You think they have a part in this?"

"Her sons are already rolling in money," Adam told her. "I don't think a few millions would make a difference."

"So money wasn't the motive?"

Adam shrugged.

"Hard to say."

"What do you mean, Adam?"

"Don't you inherit the café?" he asked.

Jenny's face changed color as she processed what Adam had said.

"You think I had something to do with it?"

"I don't think that, Jenny. But since we are talking about motives …"

"I had a generous divorce settlement. I don't need the money."

Adam leaned forward, twirling a pencil in his hand.

"You spent most of it on buying that monstrous house of yours. The café is an unexpected windfall. Admit it."

"Of course it's unexpected," Jenny cried. "You think I knew this was going to happen?"

"The Boardwalk Café is an asset you can bank on for the rest of your life."

"You know what I earned at the café last year?" Jenny asked. "Nothing! That's because I didn't take any pay. The café was barely breaking even. In fact, I put up some capital to help Petunia out."

"Did you disagree with the way Petunia was running

the café?"

"No. Why are you asking all these questions?"

"You changed the menu, didn't you? Did Petunia agree with your ideas?"

"She was a bit hesitant at first, I guess," Jenny said honestly. "But she saw how popular my food was getting. She was the one who suggested we revamp the menu."

"You're sure you didn't have any arguments with her?"

"Where is all this going, Adam?" Jenny asked, frustrated. "Why are you giving me the third degree?"

Adam sighed.

"The police are looking at you as a person of interest, Jenny."

"That's ridiculous!"

"Is it?" Adam asked. "You stood to gain by Petunia's death. You were right there at five in the morning. And you were very familiar with Petunia's routine."

"I don't have a gun."

"That's the only thing in your favor."

"You don't really think I am guilty?"

"I'm just doing my job, Jenny."

Jenny's gaze hardened as she folded her arms.

"I guess I better go get a lawyer then."

"That's a good idea," Adam agreed.

Jenny walked out without another word.

Molly was waiting for her at the Boardwalk Café. She jumped up as soon as she saw Jenny.

"Can we talk?" she asked urgently.

"Sure, Molly," Jenny said, taking her hands in hers. "What's the matter?"

Molly burst into tears.

"It's so unexpected. I don't know what to do."

"Calm down and take a deep breath," Jenny ordered. "I'm making some chamomile tea for us."

Jenny brewed tea while Molly paced in the tiny kitchen.

"What's going on? Why are you so nervous?"

Jenny took Molly by the shoulders and made her sit down.

"Tell me everything," Jenny said gently, adding honey

to their tea and placing a cup before Molly.

"I think I'm pregnant!" Molly blurted.

"That's wonderful news, Molly," Jenny said, her eyes shining with pleasure. "That's the best thing I have heard in the past few days."

"How could this happen, Jenny?"

"Do I really need to tell you that?" Jenny joked. "Have you told Chris yet?"

"No. And I'm not going to."

"Why not?"

"It's too soon, Jenny. We haven't talked about starting a family. I don't even know if he wants kids."

"Of course he wants kids," Jenny argued. "He's young and single. He's never been married. Why wouldn't he want children of his own?"

Molly considered that for a moment.

"It does seem logical," she agreed. "But what if he's mad at me for this?"

"Chris is a sensible young man," Jenny said firmly. "He's going to support you through this. I'm sure."

"We just started seeing each other," Molly mumbled.

"You love him, don't you?" Jenny asked.

"This is a big decision," Molly said, shaking her head. "I am not sure what I want myself."

"I think you should discuss this with Chris."

"I don't want him to influence me either way. Maybe I should sit on this for a while."

"Is that fair to him?"

"I don't know, Jenny," Molly said, finally taking a sip of her tea.

Jenny talked with Molly some more, forcing her to calm down. Heather burst into the café, slightly out of breath.

"I called her," Molly told Jenny.

Heather collapsed in a chair.

"Sorry I'm late. I was helping Grandma with laundry."

"Molly has some news," Jenny smiled. "Tell her, Molly."

Heather clapped her hands in glee when she heard.

"That's fantastic! Why don't you look happy, Molls?"

"She's still processing it," Jenny explained. "I was

dazed for days when I found out I was pregnant with Nick."

The girls talked for a while, trying to cheer Molly up.

"Are you coming to the town hall meeting tonight?" Heather asked them. "Barb's forming her mosquito committee."

"You mean she was serious about that whole extermination thing?" Jenny asked.

"Of course," Heather laughed. "Barb's always serious about her projects. She is asking for volunteers."

"I have my hands full at the café," Jenny said.

"That won't matter to Barb," Heather told her. "I'm sure she will rope you in one way or the other."

"That sounds ominous."

"No one in this town has ever escaped from Barb's clutches."

Jenny was tired from her long day but she forced herself to get started on the next day's prep. An hour later, she went home, her mind in turmoil. Her aunt made her famous baked macaroni and cheese for dinner.

"Where's Jimmy?" Jenny asked.

"He's having dinner with some friends tonight," Star said diplomatically.

Jenny knew that was code for a support group meeting.

"Jimmy's doing good, huh?" she asked her aunt.

Star blushed and nodded.

"Have you finalized the menu for the memorial?" she asked.

"Why don't we talk about it now?" Jenny offered. "We need all Petunia's favorite dishes. She loved my crab puffs, and the tiny pimento cheese sandwiches. We'll have fish and chips from Ethan's Crab Shack. I'll make a few salads."

"What about desserts?"

"Cupcakes and the chocolate berry cake she liked."

"People will bring food, you know," Star warned. "Get ready for a lot of casseroles."

"Have you made a guest list?"

"Oh honey," Star said sadly. "We don't need a guest list. The whole town will turn up."

"What about Vinny?"

"I expect he will turn up too," Star said.

"I can't believe she's gone," Jenny said, fighting back tears. "How are we going to survive without her?"

Chapter 7

A big black SUV with dark windows screeched to a stop in front of the Boardwalk Café. A short, skinny man wearing a red track suit and a white fedora stepped out. He tottered into the café, followed by a tall, beefy man dressed in a leather jacket. The old man sat at a window table. His companion stood behind him.

Jenny greeted the man with a smile.

"What can I get you?"

"You must be Jenny," the old man said. "Sit down."

Jenny stared back at him, mystified.

"The boss wants you to sit," the tall man repeated.

Jenny pulled out a chair and sat down.

"I'm Enzo Bellini," the old man said.

He spoke in a soft voice, almost a whisper. Jenny had to lean forward to hear his voice.

"Oh," Jenny said. "Did you know Petunia?"

The man nodded.

"She was my daughter."

His hand shook as he picked up a salt shaker and played with it.

"I know all about you," Enzo nodded. "You were good to my baby girl."

"You have it all wrong," Jenny said. "She was good to me."

"I got updates from my man here," Enzo said. "He talked to my girl every month."

"Thanks for coming for her funeral," Jenny said. "I know you probably wanted to take her home with you."

Don Enzo pulled out a cigar from his pocket. The man standing behind him lit it for him. Jenny didn't dare to tell him about the No Smoking rule.

"Don't know what she saw in this place," Enzo said. He used a string of profanities to describe the place. "But this little bitty town was home to her."

"You must have missed her all these years."

"How about some coffee?" the old man whispered, puffing on his cigar. "I hear you can bake a cake or two."

Jenny leapt up and went inside. She made a fresh pot of coffee and placed some cupcakes on a plate. She took them out to the old man.

Enzo's hand trembled as he picked up the coffee cup. Some of the dark liquid spilled over.

"I have the Parkinson's," he told Jenny. "It's supposed to get worse."

Jenny guessed the old man was well into his eighties. He was in quite good health, considering.

"Tell me about Petunia," she urged.

"Never liked that name," Enzo spat. "What kind of darn fool name is that? Her name was Leona. She was as strong and brave as a lion."

"Was she your only child?"

"The only one who gave me grandkids. My sons died long ago."

"Must have been hard to see her go."

Enzo shrugged.

"Leona, she had a mind of her own. She married young but she never liked the family business."

"What did her husband do?"

"He was my capo," Enzo said.

Jenny decided she needed to look up some mob lingo.

"Kind of like a manager," Enzo explained, guessing her thoughts. "He got gunned down."

"Oh!" Jenny stared back at Enzo, wide eyed.

"All in a day's work," Enzo said with a shrug. "Leona said it was the last straw. She wasn't having any more of it."

"How did she come to Pelican Cove? Did you know anyone here?"

"She got into the car and started driving. She trusted this guy called Fabio. He was her husband's right hand man. I made him follow her. He told me she had stopped in some small seaside town."

"It's not that far from Jersey," Jenny mused.

"It's far enough," Enzo cackled. "I bought her a house and this café. Told Fabio to stay back here and keep an eye on her."

"Did you come visit?"

Enzo shook his head mournfully.

"She didn't want to talk to me in those days. Then I

got busted. Spent twenty years in the slammer. I made Leona promise me something. She gave monthly reports to Fabio. He told me how things were going with her."

"What about her kids?"

"Leaving them was the hardest thing she ever did. She wanted them to go with her but they both refused. They were old enough to say what they wanted."

"So Vinny and his brother grew up without a mother?"

"They were already grown. Vinny was 17 when my Leona left. Baby – that's Charles, Vinny's brother - was 15."

"So there's no reason why Vinny would have a grudge against Petunia?"

"That boy is a complete idiot," Enzo hissed. "I don't trust him. I don't trust him at all."

"You think he shot Petunia?" Jenny asked with a gasp.

Enzo whistled through the gap in his teeth. "He could have. Vinny has a temper. He shoots first and asks questions later."

Jenny wondered how much she could believe the old man.

"Did Vinny know Petunia lived here in Pelican Cove?"

Enzo looked puzzled.

"I don't know."

He struggled to stand up and swayed on his feet. The henchman behind him caught him by the elbow and steadied him.

"Thank you for being there for my daughter," Enzo said to Jenny. "I won't forget it."

He shuffled out slowly and walked toward his car. The car had been running all this time with headlights on. It rolled forward as soon as Enzo slammed the door, spewing smoke in the atmosphere. Jenny stood staring after it.

"What are you staring at?" Heather tapped her on the shoulder.

"Heather!" Jenny exclaimed with a start. "I didn't see you come in."

"I'm here to assist with lunch."

"Thanks, I could really use the help."

Jenny stirred a pot of minestrone soup while Heather spooned crab salad on slices of bread. The aroma of fresh baked chocolate chip cookies wafted through the kitchen. Heather arranged two sandwiches on a plate and took a photo.

"That's for Instagram," she told Jenny. "You need to let people know you are still serving crab."

"Social media is the last thing on my mind right now," Jenny confessed.

"I know," Heather winced. "But don't forget you have a business to run, Jenny. This café is Petunia's legacy. We need to keep it alive and flourishing."

"When did you get so smart?" Jenny joked.

"I dropped the ball this past year," Heather said seriously. "I fought with Grandma, neglected the inn and dated one deadbeat after another. I'm turning over a new leaf now."

"Good for you," Jenny praised. "So what's the plan?"

"The inn hasn't been doing well," Heather shared. "I need to rebuild our brand and drum up more business. That's the first thing on my agenda."

"That's a great idea, Heather," Jenny said solemnly. "Let me know if I can help."

"I might take you up on that," Heather nodded. "We will continue to serve breakfast from the Boardwalk Café. That's not going to change. In fact, I am going to advertise it in our new brochures."

"Why don't we offer a discount to your guests?" Jenny asked eagerly. "50% off to guests of the Bayview Inn. That will help us both build business."

"Alright!" Heather crowed, giving Jenny a high five. "Now, if only we could get rid of these mosquitoes."

"You sound like Barb Norton," Jenny laughed.

"She has a point, you know," Heather said. "We had two guests check out yesterday because of the mosquitoes. Said they didn't come here to get Zika."

"That's crazy!" Jenny moaned. "Does that mean we should go volunteer for Barb's committee?"

"Didn't you hear? Barb has already dispatched her minions. They are going to inspect gardens and yards and report to her."

"Report what?"

"I guess we'll know soon enough," Heather laughed. "Barb's not going to be quiet about it."

Jenny breezed through the lunch rush with Heather's help. She packed a couple of sandwiches and cookies in a basket. It reminded her of how Petunia used to pack lunch for her and Adam. Jenny walked to the police station, hoping Adam hadn't eaten yet. She hadn't called ahead for a reason.

"Is that for me?" Adam smiled when he saw the basket on her arm. "I'm starving."

"Let's eat," Jenny nodded, unpacking a couple of plates.

She unwrapped the sandwiches and opened a packet of chips. Adam tore the plastic wrap off a dill pickle and munched on it.

"How was your meeting with the don?" he asked.

"You know about that?"

"Don Enzo or the Hawk is the head of the Bellini family. Of course we are keeping a close eye on him."

"He looks like a harmless old man."

"This harmless old man has confessed to multiple heinous crimes."

"You don't think he would harm his own daughter?"

Adam shook his head.

"He has a strong alibi. We checked."

"Have you learned anything new?"

"We found the type of gun used to shoot Petunia,"

Adam told her. "It's an advanced type. I'm sure no one in Pelican Cove owns that kind of a gun."

"Does that mean she was shot by a tourist?"

Adam was quiet. Jenny talked out loud as she ate her lunch.

"Why would a tourist do that? What motive would they have to kill Petunia?"

"You hit the nail on the head," Adam agreed. "I admit I am stumped."

"Would a mob man own that kind of gun?" Jenny asked.

"They might," Adam said. "And there's one person in town that fits the bill."

"Who is it?"

"Peter Wilson," Adam said reluctantly. "Or Fabio Lombardi. Do you know he was called The Triggerman back in the day? He was training to be a capo. He is rumored to have gunned down a dozen men once. But nothing was ever proven."

Jenny thought of the tall, quiet man she had met in the auto shop. She trembled as she imagined him holding a gun and shooting someone.

"He seemed pretty normal."

"As far as we know, Wilson gave all that up. He's been living on the straight and narrow all these years."

"So you don't suspect him at all?"

"He would have been my top suspect," Adam sighed. "But plenty of people saw him in the emergency room. He never left the building. There's no way he could have been at the beach between five and eight that morning."

"What about Vinny?" Jenny asked. "He says he was at home with his wife."

"Guys like Vinny don't get their hands dirty, Jenny. They hire people."

"What about those guys who follow him around? Six Pac or Smiley? They all carry guns."

"We are checking their alibis now."

"I wonder why Petunia's other son hasn't come here yet."

"Charles Bellini?" Adam asked. "He left the business long ago, just like Petunia. He's a school teacher out in California."

"We are not getting anywhere," Jenny said, sounding

defeated. "What if it was a tourist who was just driving through town? We will never find him."

"He will slip up somewhere," Adam promised. "We will catch him then."

"Are we meeting later tonight?" Jenny asked shyly. "It's been a while since you came for a walk on the beach."

"I've been busy," Adam said curtly. Then he gave her a wink. "But I might be heading home early tonight."

Jenny walked out of the police station, reflecting on how they seemed to have no tangible leads. Were they ever going to find out what happened to Petunia?

She decided to take the scenic route back to the café. A familiar figure squatted on the beach, scrawling something in the sand with his stick. Jenny ventured closer and greeted him.

The man stared back at her with eyes the color of the ocean.

"Hello there," she said. "You never told me your name."

"Mason," the man mumbled.

"I'm Jenny. Would you like a crab sandwich? I miscalculated and now I have plenty left over. I'll be eating them all week if you don't help me out."

"If it's no trouble," the man said, staring at his feet.

Chapter 8

Another sunny day dawned in Pelican Cove. The Magnolias stuck to their routine, silently coming to terms with their grief.

Star crumbled a blueberry muffin with her fingers and looked around at her friends. Molly was buried in a book and Betty Sue was busy knitting. Heather was fiddling with her phone as usual. Jenny stared at the ocean, a sad look in her eyes.

"Have you talked to any more people about that day?" Star asked her.

Jenny shook her head.

"The only people I talked to were regulars, people who go for a run or walk on the beach in the morning. But that doesn't include any tourists who might have been staying in town at that time."

"What about that camera?" Heather said, pointing at a spot on the roof. "Have you checked the footage for that day?"

Jenny's eyes grew wide as she turned to look up at the roof.

"I forgot all about it."

The Boardwalk Café had been the target of vandalism a few months ago. Adam had insisted they install security cameras at the front and back of the café. The camera captured a small portion of the beach adjoining the café on both sides.

"I am surprised the police haven't been here for those tapes," Molly said.

"Do you think we'll find something?" Jenny asked eagerly.

"Only one way to know," Heather said dryly. "Does that thing come with a tape of some kind?"

"Petunia insisted we get the best system available," Jenny said soberly. "It's state of the art. Uploads the video online, I think. I read the manual when we first got it but now I forgot all about it."

Heather sprang up and walked closer to the wall. She peered up at the camera and fed something into her phone.

"Give me a minute," she said. She looked up a few minutes later. "This should come with a recorder. Do you have a DVR like box somewhere? Something that looks like a DVD player?"

"I think so," Jenny said uncertainly. "Let's check in the office."

The office was nothing but a small closet that housed a computer and other knick knacks. Petunia had used the space for doing accounts and keeping track of inventory. Jenny had hardly ever gone in there, assuming it was Petunia's private domain.

Heather pointed to a black box that sat on a shelf.

"Looks like it's already hooked up to this screen."

She clicked a few more buttons and an image showed up on the screen. It was the beach at the back of the café.

"This shows footage for the past few days," Heather explained. "When do you want to go through this?"

"No time like the present," Jenny said.

Molly, Jenny and Heather squashed into the tiny office and held their breaths as the camera rolled.

A woman walking a dog came into view.

"That's the woman I spoke to," Jenny cried. "I recognize her."

The camera had captured all the people who came into range.

"Is that all you have?" Jenny asked Heather in a defeated voice. "I already talked to these people."

"We checked the camera for one day before and after, just in case. I'm sorry, Jenny. This is all we have."

Molly seemed thoughtful.

"This camera only captures a certain portion of the beach, right? And the bench Petunia sat on is to the right. What about people who might have approached the bench from the other side?"

Heather caught on immediately.

"You need to check if anyone else uses security cameras," she told Jenny. "Talk to the other store owners."

"That sounds like a plan," Jenny said hopefully. "Wanna go with me?"

Molly and Heather both eagerly accepted. The girls were back at the Boardwalk Café half an hour later, looking disappointed.

"Any luck?" Star and Betty Sue asked.

"None of them have surveillance cameras," Jenny groaned.

"I could have told you that," Betty Sue said stiffly. "But you went off without saying a word to us."

"Most people don't lock doors around here, sweetie,"

Star reasoned. "They would never think of mounting security cameras."

"Petunia got spooked by that attack on the café," Betty Sue said. "That's the only reason she went for that doohickey up there. That and because you wanted to impress that Hopkins boy."

"That's not true," Jenny objected.

Star and Betty Sue ignored her.

"I wonder why Adam hasn't advised everyone on Main Street to go for a security system," Heather cribbed. "Just imagine ... if there had been a camera mounted on every shop, we might have caught Petunia's killer red handed."

"Forget the cameras," Star said. "Did you talk to the people who own these shops? Maybe they saw someone suspicious?"

"I talked to some of them," Jenny told her. "There's one guy I haven't talked to. Remember that little snow cone place by the big parking lot? It was closed when I went by."

"That place might be shut up for the season," Star told her. "It's owned by a couple who live in the city. They have a cottage here. They open that store when they live here in the summer."

"I think they are still around," Molly spoke up. "Chris and I got a snow cone from there just yesterday."

"I'll go there later today," Jenny promised the women.

The Magnolias were taking turns helping Jenny at the café. It was Star's turn to stay in and help with lunch.

Jenny was making barbecued chicken wings with potato salad. It could get messy but people loved it. She grilled some corn on the cob and slathered it with her special herbed butter.

Vinny and his posse came in and sat out on deck. They ate double helpings of everything and asked for dessert. Jenny took half a strawberry cheesecake out to them.

Vinny kissed his fingers with a smacking sound.

"My Ma knew what she was doing. Your food is just yum."

"Thanks," Jenny said with a shrug. "Your mother was very nice to me."

"Any luck finding out what happened?" Vinny asked. "Hey, you meet some wise guy who won't talk, just let me know. The boys will make sure he opens up."

"I'll keep that in mind," Jenny promised.

Jenny prepped for next morning before she closed the café for the day. She walked to the snow cone shop, praying she could talk to the owners. The little kiosk was closed again. A man sat on the floor, leaning against it, reading a book. He sat on a sleeping bag which had seen better days.

"Any idea when they might open?" she asked him.

The man looked up at her and shook his head.

"Reckon they are gone for a while."

"Do you come here often?" Jenny asked him.

He gave a slight nod and went back to reading his book.

Jenny inched a bit closer to the man.

"Can I ask you a few questions, please?"

"I don't want any trouble," the man said slowly. "I'm just sitting here reading a book."

"You can sit here as long as you want," Jenny said hastily. "I don't mind that."

The man quirked an eyebrow and waited for her to go on.

"There was an incident here a few days ago," Jenny

began.

"You talking about that old woman who got shot?"

"You know about that?" Jenny asked in a rush.

"Was right here, wasn't I?" the man said. "Heard a woman screaming her head off. Got up to see what was wrong. Turns out there's a dead woman sitting on that bench over there."

"Were you here the night before that?"

"I don't sleep here, lady," the man dismissed. "Got here a bit after five. I like to catch the first rays of the morning sun."

"Did you see anyone else around here?"

"A man was leaving around the time I got here."

"Can you describe him?" Jenny asked eagerly, holding her breath.

The man shook his head.

"Not really. I just saw his back. He got into a car and drove away."

"Did he come from the beach?"

"No idea," the man shrugged.

"What kind of car was he driving? Did you notice the tags?"

"I was barely awake," the man reasoned. "It was some kind of dark car. A sedan, I think. That's all I can tell you."

"Were there any other cars in the lot?"

"I don't think so," the man said. "Can I read my book now?"

Jenny thanked the man for his time.

"Why don't you come to the Boardwalk Café sometime? Lunch is on me."

The man's face broke into a smile and he agreed readily.

Jenny walked home, trying to process what the man had told her. Her heart thudded when she realized he might have spotted the murderer.

Jenny and Star spent a quiet evening at home, watching television. Jenny pulled herself out of bed at four thirty the next morning and got ready to go to the café.

The Boardwalk Café seemed lonely without Petunia's presence. Trying to drum up some inspiration, Jenny decided to mix things up for breakfast. She made a batch of blueberry banana muffins with sliced almonds.

"On the house," she told Captain Charlie when he came in for breakfast. "It's a new recipe I'm trying."

"Anything you bake is going to be good for me," he told her.

A couple came in and sat at a window table. The man was dressed in khakis and a light blue shirt. The woman wore a dress Jenny knew cost three figures.

They ordered the breakfast special. The man buried his head in a newspaper and the woman looked around with a sneer on her face.

Vinny and his guys came in for breakfast. Vinny gave a start when he spotted the couple. He walked up to the man and slapped him on the back.

"Didn't know you were coming, Baby," he roared.

The man dropped his newspaper and looked up at Vinny.

"Of course I came," he said. "She was my mother too."

Vinny summoned Jenny to the table.

"Have you met my brother, sweetheart?" Vinny asked, pulling up a chair and sitting between the couple.

The woman looked at him as if he was vermin. Vinny ignored her.

Jenny greeted the man seated at the table. Outwardly, he was nothing like Vinny. But there was a clear family resemblance. They both had a cleft chin and brown eyes the same color as Petunia's.

"You look a lot like your mother," Jenny told him.

Heather came in with an empty basket on her arm.

"Sorry I'm late." She pulled out a tray of muffins from the oven and started placing them in the basket.

"What's going on outside?" she asked, peeping out of the kitchen. She clutched Jenny's arm when she spotted the couple. "See that woman? She was here before."

"In the café? You must be mistaken, Heather. She just came in with her husband."

"Not in the café," Heather said, wide eyed. "In Pelican Cove."

"Are you sure? That guy is Vinny's brother. The woman's his wife, I guess."

"What's their name?"

"Bellini, of course. Why?"

"That's not the name she gave me."

Jenny stared at Heather with her hands on her hips.

"You must be mistaken. Charles was just telling Vinny they came in last night."

"That Charles guy did check in last night," Heather confirmed. "But the wife was in town before this. I'm telling you she stayed at the inn. She checked in with a different name though."

"That doesn't make sense."

"Wait till you hear the rest," Heather said under her breath. "She was here when Petunia got shot. She was right here in Pelican Cove, under an assumed name."

Jenny's eyes gleamed in triumph.

"That's a whole new can of worms, Heather."

Chapter 9

Adam Hopkins was engrossed in some urgent paperwork. Jenny sat in his office at the police station, tapping her foot impatiently.

"How much longer, Adam?" she burst out.

"Unfortunately, I don't work for you," he told Jenny curtly. "Come back later or wait till I finish what I'm doing."

Jenny chose to wait.

Adam finally pushed aside the stack of files and gave a big yawn.

"What have you done now, Jenny? Why are you here?"

"I have a witness," Jenny said eagerly. "He might have seen the killer leave the scene of the crime."

"Does this witness have a name?"

"I guess," Jenny said. "I didn't ask him."

"What does he do?"

"He was sitting in that big parking lot, reading a book."

"So you are relying on the word of some transient who

could be anywhere right now."

"I think you'll find him at the same spot," Jenny persisted. "Right by the snow cone shop."

"That little hut?" Adam asked sardonically. "That's closed for the season."

"You don't have to go in there. You have to talk to the guy who sits outside."

"Okay. What did this guy say?"

"He saw someone get into a car that morning. Don't you see? This guy could be our shooter."

"What kind of car was it?" Adam asked.

"He didn't say," Jenny admitted. "It was dark. He thinks it was a sedan."

"That's slim, Jenny. What am I supposed to do with this information?"

"Follow up," Jenny shrugged. "Isn't that what the police do? Spread your net wider, Adam. I am sure someone else must have seen that car that morning."

"I'll look into it, Jenny," Adam sighed. "No promises though."

"I understand," Jenny nodded sadly.

Adam leaned forward and looked into her eyes.

"What are you doing tonight? How about getting dinner somewhere?"

Jenny's heart skipped a beat. Adam had asked her to move in with him a few months ago. He had been curt with her after she refused. They hadn't been on a proper date since then.

"I can manage that," she said. "Will you pick me up at home?"

"You're on," Adam said, trying to hide a smile.

Jenny hurried back to the café. Star and Heather were assembling sandwiches in the kitchen.

"Who's that grin for?" Heather asked immediately. "Tell me, quick."

"I'm having dinner with Adam."

"Finally!" Star exclaimed, rolling her eyes. "Looks like that boy is coming to his senses."

"Just roll with it," Heather advised. "Stay away from taboo topics."

"I'll try," Jenny agreed.

She dressed carefully that evening, not sure where her

relationship was headed. Was it just dinner between friends, or did Adam want to pick up where they left off. She wished he had given her a hint.

Adam arrived on time, dressed in a sports coat. Jenny was glad she hadn't worn jeans. He was wearing his favorite shirt, one she had bought for him. She had chosen it for its color, the exact shade of blue as his eyes.

"Have fun," Star called out merrily. "I won't wait up."

"We are going to Virginia Beach," Adam told her. "There's a new seafood restaurant on the boardwalk. It's getting rave reviews."

"Sounds great," Jenny said enthusiastically.

"We haven't gone out in a while," Adam explained. "I wanted this evening to be special."

Jenny slipped her hand in his and clutched it tight. Adam was a grouch most of the time but he did manage to surprise her sometimes.

They talked about the weather and their kids. They were both careful about avoiding painful topics.

Jenny enjoyed the drive over the Chesapeake Bay Bridge-Tunnel. The road was busier than usual with the last of the summer tourists.

The hostess led them to a table on the beach. Adam ordered Jenny's favorite local wine along with the shrimp cocktail. The food lived up to the hype. They both got the blackened fish and watched the people walking by. Vinny waved at her from a table at the other end. Enzo sat next to him, wearing a blue tracksuit, puffing his cigar. Charles was the third person at the table.

"Looks like a family dinner," Jenny noted.

Smiley and the other guys occupied a table adjoining Vinny's.

"Forget about them," Adam said. "This is our night."

"What do you want to talk about?" Jenny asked.

Adam pulled out a tiny box from his pocket. He handed it to Jenny.

"What is it?" Jenny asked with bated breath.

"Open it," Adam smiled.

Jenny flipped the box open and felt herself relax. The box held a pair of pearl earrings.

"They are beautiful," Jenny breathed. "But what's the occasion? It's not my birthday or anything."

"I wanted to do something special for you," Adam

said.

"You know you don't have to buy me expensive gifts, Adam," Jenny said frankly.

"Do you like them?"

"Of course I like them. They are cute."

"Then they are yours," Adam said.

He took Jenny's hands in his and kissed them.

"I missed you, Jenny."

"I missed you too," Jenny said quickly.

"Let's not fight about anything. I don't care where you live. Your house, my house. You have a place in my heart, Jenny King."

Jenny felt her eyes fill up.

"Don't make me cry, Adam Hopkins."

"Never," Adam said, shaking his head. "I want to make you happy for the rest of your days."

"Just be yourself, Adam," Jenny whispered. "That's enough for me."

They ordered baked Alaska for dessert and shared it, feeding each other.

"Shall we go for a walk here?" Adam asked, offering Jenny his arm.

Jenny blushed and nodded. She wished she could stay in that moment forever, without thinking about the other things going on in her life. But Vinny's presence was a stark reminder of what had happened to her friend. She wasn't going to give up until Petunia's killer was behind bars.

Jenny had a spring in her step as she entered the Boardwalk Café the next morning. A smile tugged at the corner of her mouth as she relived the evening she had spent with Adam. She made a special streusel topping for the muffins and chatted animatedly with her customers.

Molly and Heather teased her mercilessly. Star and Betty Sue laughed at their antics.

"I'm going to be a bridesmaid soon," Heather crowed.

"Don't get ahead of yourself, girl," Jenny said shyly.

She was wearing the pearl earrings Adam had given her.

Barb Norton huffed up the café steps and flopped into a chair.

"You're coming tonight, aren't you?" she asked. "No excuses."

"What are you doing now, Barb?" Betty Sue asked.

"Pelican Cove has a big problem," Barb announced. "No wonder we are battling this mosquito menace. We are going to address it all in tonight's meeting."

"There's a town hall tonight?" Heather asked. "Great. I have been working on some off-season discounts at the Bayview Inn for the locals. I want to talk about them at the meeting."

"We may not have time for frivolous stuff," Barb dismissed. "See you later, girls."

Barb declined Jenny's offer of coffee and muffins and went on her way.

"I'm sure this has to do with those inspections," Molly said.

She turned out to be right.

Most of the town had flocked to the town hall meeting. People didn't look too pleased to be there. Jenny decided Barb had managed to browbeat all of them into attending.

Barb tapped on the mic and called for attention.

"You have been negligent, Pelican Cove. You have all been negligent."

A murmur rose through the crowd. A wisecrack or two followed and everyone began laughing.

"This is not funny," Barb said. "The Extermination Committee inspected every garden and yard in town. Their results are very disturbing."

"Get on with it, Barb," Betty Sue bellowed from the front row.

"60% of the people in town have standing water. Some of you have bird feeders overflowing with water, others have gutters full of rain water ... and the ponds and ditches. These are breeding grounds for mosquitoes."

"What do we do now?" someone asked.

"We need to spray the town," Barb said. "But we don't have funds. I am open to any fund raising ideas."

Jenny tuned out Barb's voice and thought about Petunia. There hadn't been a single positive development in the case. Were they missing something obvious?

She thought of the woman staying at Heather's inn. Jenny decided to talk to her the next day.

Laura Bellini helped her by coming in for breakfast by herself the next morning. She ordered the crab omelet with a smirk and sat drumming her fingers on the table.

"We need to talk," Jenny announced.

"Is that a small town thing?" the woman sneered. "Talking to every customer?"

"Petunia meant a lot to me," Jenny said curtly. "You are her son's wife, aren't you?"

The woman gave a slight nod.

"Why did you check into the Bayview Inn under a false name?"

The woman's smile slipped. She looked around fearfully and placed a finger on her lips.

"Can we keep that between us? Please?"

Jenny noticed how Laura's posture changed. She was on edge.

"Why did you do it? Tell me everything."

Laura cut a piece of her omelet and chewed it slowly. Her eyes narrowed as she looked at Jenny.

"Tell me how you knew my mother-in-law."

"I am new in town," Jenny said. "I was at a loose end, looking for work. Petunia took me in. She was good to me."

"Wait. Are you that woman who inherited this café?" Laura asked. "Charles told me some upstart woman had sweet talked his mother into it."

"I didn't ask for it," Jenny told her. "I had no idea she was going to do that."

"She talked about you a lot," Laura said. "Said you were like the daughter she never had."

"When did you talk to Petunia?" Jenny asked, surprised.

"When I came to town earlier this month," Laura Bellini explained.

"Why did you come here, exactly?"

"You know what my husband does?" she asked Jenny.

"I hear he is not part of the family business," Jenny said haltingly.

"He's a teacher!" Laura exclaimed with disgust. "He's a teacher in the public school system. You know what that job pays? A pittance."

"But your husband is rich, right?" Jenny asked.

"His grandpa wrote him off when we moved to California. I have to scrimp and save when his family is rolling in billions."

"That must be hard on you," Jenny commiserated.

"Darn right it is," Laura swore.

She had the family habit of using plenty of expletives in her speech.

"I want a better life, you know," Laura said, pulling a cigarette out of her purse.

"There's no smoking here," Jenny said quickly.

"Relax," Laura snapped. "I'm not going to light it."

She placed the cigarette between her lips and mumbled under her breath.

"I want a better life," she repeated, pulling the cigarette out of her mouth. "I want to drive a better car. I want to wear good clothes. I want our kids to go to a private school."

"You have kids?" Jenny asked in awe. "Did Petunia know she had grandchildren?"

"She knew," Laura said softly. "She walked out on the family a long time ago."

"Why did you think she would talk to you?"

"I was here to beg for money," Laura confessed. "It was like a last resort. I didn't tell Charles where I was going. I wasn't even sure she would agree to talk to me. That's why I used a false name."

"What did she say?" Jenny asked.

"She asked me how much I wanted," Laura said with wonder. "All that tension I was feeling was for nothing. She offered me a cool million. Told me to buy something nice for the kids. One million dollars. Can you believe it? I've never seen that kind of money."

Another string of profanity followed.

"That's just the tip of the iceberg, though, isn't it?" Jenny asked. "Your husband inherits several million dollars now that she is gone."

Chapter 10

Sun worshippers lined the beach behind the Boardwalk Café, sprawled on colorful beach towels. The weather was a balmy eighty degrees. Pelican Cove remained an attractive choice for tourists even in September.

Molly sat on the café's deck with a frown on her face, surrounded by the Magnolias.

"This is great news," Star was saying. "Why haven't you told us before?"

"A baby," Betty Sue said softly, her needles clacking as she knit a blue colored scarf. "That's exactly what we need."

"Ask her if she has told Chris yet though?" Heather interrupted. "What does he feel about this?"

"I talked to Chris," Molly told them.

"And?" Four voices chorused.

"He wants to get married right away."

"Excellent," Star boomed.

Jenny added her congratulations.

"I knew that boy would do the right thing," Betty Sue

thundered.

"But I don't want to," Molly burst out. "At least, not this way."

"What do you mean, Molls?" Jenny asked.

"I have been married before," Molly reminded them. "It turned out to be a mistake. I don't want to get carried away this time."

"You love Chris, don't you?" Heather asked suspiciously.

"Of course I do," Molly said vigorously. "But does he love me enough?"

"What nonsense!" Star exclaimed. "I've seen how that boy looks at you."

"You already met the parents," Heather reminded her.

"I don't want a shotgun wedding," Molly said, warding them off. "This way, I am forcing his hand. I will never know if Chris really loves me. Or rather, if he loves me enough."

Jenny guessed what Molly was trying to say.

"There are no secrets between us, Molly," she said. "I think it's best if you clear the air."

Star and Betty Sue gave each other a knowing look.

"What's going on?" Heather asked, mystified.

"Molly thinks Chris might still have feelings for you," Jenny said flatly.

"What?" Heather asked, wide eyed. "That's ridiculous."

Heather and Chris had been a couple for several years. Everyone knew they had an understanding. A year ago, Heather had decided to date other people. She paraded one guy after another before Chris. He had decided Heather wasn't coming back. He fell in love with Molly, Heather's gentle, soft spoken friend.

"I know he still cares about you," Molly persisted. "And he worries about you."

"Chris and I have known each other since third grade," Heather said. "I hope we will always be close. But he's not in love with me now, Molly. Trust me."

Jenny noticed how Heather avoided saying anything about her own feelings.

"He's very excited," Molly finally said with a smile. "He insists on going with me to the doctor."

"Chris will make a wonderful father," Jenny assured her. "Don't overanalyze things, Molly."

"I guess I'm being silly," Molly said grudgingly. "I'm lucky to have him."

"She's already getting emotional," Star cackled. "She'll be puking her guts out in a few days."

"I didn't have any morning sickness at all," Betty Sue shared. "Don't worry, Molly. We'll take care of you."

"I know you will," Molly said tearfully. "You're the best friends a girl could ask for."

They huddled together for a group hug. Star voiced what everyone was thinking.

"I can't believe she's gone."

"She's alive in our heart," Betty Sue sniffed. She blew her nose in a lace handkerchief and looked at Jenny. "Do you have any suspects at all?"

Jenny looked beaten.

"Every person I talk to seems to have an alibi."

"What about that boy who goes around wearing that ridiculous hat?"

"Vinny? He inherits millions. But he was home in New Jersey the day Petunia was shot."

"Don't these people hire hit men?" Star said.

"That's true. But I don't think Vinny had anything to do with it."

"You're not crushing after this mobster, are you?" Heather giggled.

Jenny silenced her with a glare.

"I think Peter Wilson could have done it."

"That car mechanic?" Star asked. "All those times I took my car to him, I never knew he was in the mafia."

"Peter Wilson was meeting Petunia that morning," Jenny reminded them. "He knew exactly where she was going to be at a certain time."

"What's his alibi?"

"He was in the hospital with a sick child. I suppose he could have crept out for a few minutes. But Adam is sure he was there all the time."

"What about that couple staying at our inn?" Heather asked.

"Laura Bellini," Jenny nodded. "She was here to ask Petunia for money. I don't trust that woman."

"Is that all you have done until now?" Betty Sue complained. "What about finding someone who was on the beach that day?"

"I did talk to some beach walkers," Jenny said. "They couldn't tell me much. But this guy in the parking lot sounds more promising. I am going to follow up that lead."

A familiar voice trilled in the background.

"Yooohooo …" Barb Norton called out, puffing up the café steps.

"Why are you here, Barb?" Star asked curtly.

"We need funds for the aerial spraying of the town," Barb wheezed. "Surely you heard that at yesterday's meeting?"

"Go on," Betty Sue said reluctantly.

"I have an idea. We are going to impose fines on people who have standing water or ponds on their properties. They have directly contributed to the mosquito menace. So they should be the ones who have to pay."

"Are you out of your mind?" Betty Sue cried. "You can't fine people just because they haven't cleaned out their gutters."

"I can," Barb beamed. "I went through town regulations. And I found the legal loophole which allows me to levy those fines."

"People are not going to like it," Heather said.

"You are one of those people," Barb said maliciously. "That lily pond you have is a breeding ground for the deadliest mosquitoes."

"Can't you raise money any other way?" Jenny asked.

"I'm glad you asked," Barb said. "I am thinking of a bake sale. I will need your help with that."

"I'm already stretched thin, Barb," Jenny protested. "I don't think I can contribute much this time."

"We'll see about that," Barb said.

She stood up and pointed a finger at Betty Sue.

"My volunteers are printing up notices as we speak. You have three days to pay the fine. Otherwise you will have to pay double."

"What …" Betty Sue sputtered. "You're out of control, Barb!"

Barb Norton gave them a jaunty wave and walked down the beach.

"She's going to come to a sticky end one of these days," Star said. "Mark my words."

"I'm not paying any atrocious fines," Betty Sue

declared. "I don't care what Barb says."

The Magnolias dispersed after that.

Star insisted on staying back to help Jenny. A man came into the café an hour later. Star was at the counter.

"Can I help you?"

"I'm looking for someone," he mumbled. "A lady told me I could come here for lunch."

Jenny came out of the kitchen just then. She recognized the man who had been reading in the parking lot.

"I got this," she told her aunt.

She greeted the man and showed him to a table. She was back with a big bowl of chicken noodle soup.

"Grilled cheese sandwiches for lunch today," she told him. "Is that okay?"

The man nodded, looking hungrily at the soup. He picked up his spoon and began eating. Jenny kept an eye on him. She was back with a hot crispy sandwich oozing melted cheese.

"You're a good cook," the man told her. "This soup is just like the one my grandma used to make. She always had soup on the stove in the fall."

"I'll pack some more for you," Jenny said.

"I remembered something," the man said suddenly.

"Is this about the man you saw in the parking lot?" Jenny asked eagerly.

"No. But it's about the car. It had a big dent on one side. And some kind of sticker on the back window."

"Good catch," Jenny beamed. "That's a huge help. Thanks so much."

The man blushed.

"Someone told me the woman who died was your friend. Just trying to help."

"I appreciate it," Jenny said. "You are welcome here anytime."

Jenny handed him a brown paper bag when he got up to leave. She had added a container of soup and some muffins from that morning. She hoped he would get at least one more meal out of it.

Jenny had just turned her back to go into the kitchen when a familiar voice called out to her.

"Jason!" she exclaimed in delight. "I was going to call

you."

"My 2 PM cancelled," he said. "Thought I would enjoy a leisurely lunch at my favorite café."

Star came out and hugged Jason.

"Jenny hasn't eaten yet either. Why don't you two sit out on deck? I'll get your lunch."

"You're looking chipper today," Jenny observed as they ate their soup.

Jason shrugged.

"It's a beautiful day and we are lucky to be alive and kicking."

Jason had been dealing with a bad breakup. Jenny realized he was finally coming out of his shell.

"Ready to put on your sleuthing cap?" she asked.

"Bring it on," Jason nodded.

Jenny told him about the man in the parking lot and what he had seen.

"We need to figure out where that car went," Jason said thoughtfully. "Why don't we go to the parking lot after lunch?"

They drove down Main Street in Jason's fancy car.

Jenny relaxed in the heated seats. She had forgotten how comfortable they could be.

Jason made a right first. It took them back toward the Boardwalk Café. Jason drove past the cluster of stores. The road wound across town for a mile before ending in a cluster of homes. They were expensive properties right on the water with their own private docks. Jason and Jenny could see a boat tied to many of them.

"This is a dead end," Jason said. "Let's go the other way."

They turned around and drove past the parking lot. The road stretched on for a couple of miles and eventually merged on the bridge that connected the island to the main shore.

"What about those lanes we saw?" Jenny asked, referring to a couple of turnoffs they had encountered.

Jason obliged her by driving down the lanes. Both of them were deserted and ended in a small clearing of sorts.

"Looks like he drove out of town," Jason mused.

"How can you be so sure?"

"I'm just speculating, Jenny," Jason admitted. "He couldn't have gone back into town. He could have gone into one of those lanes to hide. But why would he do that? He would want to get out of town as soon as possible."

"If only someone saw where that car went ..."

"We can check security cameras," Jason told her. "They might have recorded the car driving by."

"I spoke to some store owners around the café," Jenny told him. "None of them have cameras."

"The Newburys have cameras," Jason said suddenly. "Remember that warehouse we passed? It belongs to them."

"Will they give us access?" Jenny asked.

"They can't refuse," Jason said.

He pulled up at the warehouse a few minutes later. The security guy on duty recognized him. Jenny explained what they were looking for.

"I can't give you access without getting approval," he said.

"We just want to look," Jenny told him. "If we find something, I will go talk to Julius Newbury myself."

Jenny and Jason squashed into the cramped security office and waited for the man to pull up the relevant footage. There had been no cars on the road that morning.

"How is that possible?" Jenny wailed. "Where did the car go?"

"He could have parked the car in the woods and walked somewhere," Jason suggested. "He's had plenty of time since then to go back and move the car."

"We are never going to find him," Jenny said in a defeated voice.

"We can't do more than this, Jenny," Jason reasoned. "Let the police handle it."

"I told Adam about this," Jenny said soberly. "He ticked me off."

"So we'll talk to him again. My gut tells me this car is important, Jenny. We need to find it anyhow."

Chapter 11

Jenny finished serving breakfast at the Boardwalk Café and walked to the police station with her fingers crossed. She wanted to get an update from Adam. She had no idea how forthcoming he would be. It all depended on his mood.

"Anything new?" she asked, taking a seat before him.

Adam was struggling with a bottle of pain pills. Jenny unscrewed the bottle and handed him two pills.

"Nothing much to share," Adam told her. "At least, nothing I care to tell you, Jenny."

"How kind," Jenny said, her voice dripping with sarcasm.

"You can leave now."

"Not so fast, Adam. Have you run a background check on Charles Bellini?"

"The other son? He's a middle school teacher. Teaches English and history, I think."

"And his wife?"

"What about her?"

"Does she have a job? What does she do?"

Adam hesitated.

"We haven't given her much importance."

"Maybe you should," Jenny told him. "She's devious. She stayed at the Bayview Inn under an assumed name."

"Who told you that?" Adam asked.

"Heather did. And Laura Bellini told me so herself."

"When was this?"

"She was right here the day Petunia died," Jenny said triumphantly. "What do you think of that?"

Adam leaned forward with interest.

"I did not know that. Good work, Jenny."

"I guess we have Heather to thank for the heads up."

Jenny told Adam about her conversation with Laura Bellini.

"If she had anything to hide, she wouldn't have come back here," Adam mused.

"She could be stupid," Jenny offered. "Or overconfident."

"You don't like her, I guess."

"She said some nasty things about Petunia."

"You can't let that cloud your judgment," Adam advised. "Laura as a person is not on trial here."

"You're right, I guess," Jenny admitted.

"Am I seeing you later tonight?" Adam asked. "Tank misses you."

Tank was Adam's yellow Labrador. He had traveled with Adam on his various deployments. Tank and Jenny had taken a shine to each other. When Jenny's husband had cruelly retained custody of her own aging dog, she had been heartbroken. Tank had filled the void a bit.

"I miss him too. Why don't you let him visit? Let him stay at Seaview for a few days. Star and I would love to pamper him a bit."

"I'm sure he will love that," Adam smiled.

Neither of them talked about Adam coming to stay. Adam had spent a few months at Seaview when his own home was being renovated. He wanted Jenny to move in with him after that but she had refused to leave her home. Jenny didn't know how they would ever move past that issue.

"You are sure the police have made no progress?" Jenny wheedled. "Why don't you throw me some scraps, Adam?"

"You're relentless, aren't you?" Adam shook his head in wonder.

"I plan to badger you until you give up and spill the beans."

Adam gave a deep sigh and leaned back in his chair.

"We might have something," Adam said reluctantly. "Most people have talked about a white guy wearing a hooded jacket. He was seen around the beach."

"Where on the beach?" Jenny pounced.

"Near the bench," Adam admitted.

"What else? Did they notice the color of his hair? Anything else?"

"There wasn't much light so it's hard to say. They did mention seeing some kind of picture on the back of the jacket."

"You mean like a logo?"

"A drawing or a graphic of some kind. This is where it gets distorted. One person says it looked like a skull. Another said it looked like a big bird."

"An eagle?" Jenny asked thoughtfully.

"More like a turkey."

"What else?"

"We have been looking around for a man wearing that jacket."

"What if he was a tourist?" Jenny asked with a frown. "He must be long gone."

"Question is, what was this guy doing on the beach so early in the morning."

"Could he be the one who got into the car and drove away?"

"No idea, Jenny," Adam said.

He banged a fist on the table, looking frustrated.

"I knew Petunia longer than you, Jenny. You think I don't want to find out what happened to her? I'm doing everything I can to find her killer."

Jenny patted his hand.

"I know you're good at your job, Adam. I trust you."

Jenny dragged herself back to the café. Star was stirring a big pot of soup for lunch.

"How's the chili?" Jenny asked.

"Just yum," Star said, tasting some with a spoon. "I measured out the ingredients for the corn bread."

"I'm going to start mixing it," Jenny said. "Let me grab a cup of coffee first."

"Are you going to add jalapenos?"

Jenny nodded, thinking of her son Nick.

"Nicky loves my jalapeno cornbread," she said wistfully. "He's been eating it since he was six. He never complained about the heat."

Jenny rubbed a tiny gold heart shaped charm hanging around her neck on a chain. Her son Nick had gifted her a charm every year for Mother's Day. She wore them around her neck now, close to her heart. They provided the only tangible connection she had with her child.

"When is that scamp coming home?" Star asked. "Have you talked to him recently?"

Jenny shook her head.

"I haven't told him about Petunia. She adored him."

"You should call him, Jenny," Star said. "He needs to know."

Jenny and her aunt talked about how Nick was growing up to be a fine young man. Jenny pulled the first batch of corn bread out of the oven. She cut a generous piece and broke it in half. She offered it to her aunt.

"Delicious," Star said, fanning her mouth. "Better save some for us. You're going to run out of this in no time."

Jenny smiled and ladled chili into a big soup bowl. She garnished it with some chopped green onions and shredded cheddar cheese. A dollop of sour cream went on top. Jenny placed a piece of corn bread on one side and began taking pictures.

"For the Internet?" her aunt asked.

There was a commotion of sorts outside. Jenny heard raised voices and ran to see what was happening.

Barb Norton sat at a table, her chest heaving. One side of her face was caked with mud. A tiny trickle of blood flowed down her forehead.

"Barb!" Jenny cried. "What happened to you?"

"I was attacked," Barb wailed dramatically. "That's what happened. In broad daylight, no less. What's this town coming to?"

Star had come out of the kitchen behind Jenny.

"Calm down, Barb," she said. "You are going to blow a gasket."

Barb's red face turned purple.

"I'm not going to calm down," she cried. "I almost lost my life."

Jenny poured water in a glass and made Barb drink it.

"I'm making tea," she said. "Why don't you come into the kitchen and tell us what happened?"

"Call your boyfriend," Barb commanded. "I want to file a complaint."

"I can call the police from the kitchen," Jenny assured her. "Let's take care of you first."

Barb's story was simple enough. She had been walking on the road, going to the library. She didn't know what hit her. She blacked out and when she came to, she was lying in a ditch by the side of the road. A man walking by had helped her up.

"First Petunia, now me. Do you think someone is targeting older ladies?"

Jenny didn't have an answer for that. She called Adam at the police station and told him what had happened.

"He's coming here," she told Barb.

Adam arrived ten minutes later, looking grim. Barb bombarded him with a string of questions.

"Let me ask the questions, please," Adam said. "You do want me to write up a report?"

Adam learned that Barb had been walking on a lonely stretch of road. She hadn't seen anyone else.

Jenny spotted a bump at the back of Barb's head. She hadn't noticed it before.

"You need to go to the doctor, Barb," Jenny said. "Get checked out."

Adam offered to drive Barb to the emergency room at the hospital. She agreed readily.

"What do you think of that?" Jenny asked her aunt after they left.

Heather rushed in just then, waving a piece of paper in the air.

"I want to kill Barb Norton!"

"Apparently, you are not the only one," Jenny said.

Heather barely heard her.

"Just look at this, Jenny. Look at how atrocious this fine is that she is asking us to pay."

Jenny took the paper from Heather and gasped as she saw the amount at the bottom of the page.

"What is this for?"

"According to her, the Bayview Inn has contributed to the mosquito menace. This is her way of punishing us for it."

"It does sound a bit much," Jenny agreed.

"That's not all," Heather continued in an incensed voice. "She wants to destroy our lily pond. My Dad and I dug that pond when I was little. It's not just a pond, Jenny. It has memories attached to it."

"Are you the only one who got this kind of notice?" Jenny asked.

"I bet we got one too," Star said drily. "Barb's going to take objection to your water fountain. I'm sure of it."

"That fountain's not going anywhere," Jenny said stoutly.

She looked at Heather.

"Well?"

"These notices have been served all around town," Heather said. "She's even sent one to the Newburys. Ada was on the phone with Grandma."

The Newburys were the richest people in town. They considered themselves a notch above the rest.

"She has guts. I'll give her that."

"She's being idiotic," Star said flatly. "There are other ways to raise money. I think Barb Norton has gone too far this time."

Jenny's eyes widened as she processed her aunt's words.

"You don't think she was attacked because of these fines?"

Star shrugged.

"You can only push people so far."

Heather was looking puzzled. Jenny explained what had happened.

"No way," Heather said. "The people of Pelican Cove don't go around attacking each other."

There was a flurry of footsteps outside and a figure in a leather jacket peeped in.

"Boss wants his lunch."

"I'll be out in a minute, Smiley," Jenny said.

"You know those mobsters by name?" Heather asked,

rolling her eyes.

"Do you think one of them might have hit Barb?" Star asked.

Jenny gave it some thought.

"I don't think Vinny cares about the mosquitoes."

She served the chili into bowls and placed the cheese and onions on small plates. She cut big pieces of corn bread and served them on a platter.

Vinny took one bite of the chili and smacked his lips appreciatively.

"This is so good! You sure know how to cook."

"I'm planning the menu for Petunia's memorial. Is there something you want to add?"

"Ma liked those tiny meatballs on a stick," Vinny said. "She made them for all our birthdays."

"I didn't know that," Jenny told him. "I'll put them on the menu."

She looked at Vinny and debated what she was going to say next.

"Petunia didn't say much. Was she always that quiet?"

"She might have acted like a mouse. But she had the

heart of a lion. She knew what she wanted and she went after it."

Jenny brought out plates of tiramisu. She had never served it in the café before.

"It's your mother's recipe," she told Vinny. "She had written it down at the back of a diary."

"This is our Nona's recipe," Vinny said after he had tasted it. "Our grandmother's. Ma was making this the day our Pa got whacked."

Jenny understood why Petunia had never made it again.

Chapter 12

Molly came up the steps of the café and sat down with a sigh. She put her feet up on a chair and dug into a warm muffin. Star and Betty Sue exchanged a knowing look when Molly reached for her second one.

"What?" she pouted. "I'm just hungry."

"And you're eating for two," Betty Sue said, her eyes gleaming. "When do you go to the doctor?"

"Tomorrow. Chris is going with me."

"Of course he is," Betty Sue said. "That there is a responsible boy. He'll do right by you, Molly."

"I am able to take care of myself and my baby," Molly protested. "I don't need to be taken care of."

"Okay, okay." Star held up her hand. "We know you girls like to think you can do everything alone. And that's admirable. But be happy you have a guy like Chris."

"I am," Molly said emphatically. "Why do you think I am in love with him?"

She blushed prettily and picked up her cup of coffee.

"Switch to ginger ale," Betty Sue said. "That's better for you."

"I can't imagine giving up coffee," Molly said stoutly.

"Who's giving up what?" Jenny asked, coming out with six steaming hot muffins on a plate.

Heather was right behind her.

"Pumpkin and cream cheese muffins," Jenny announced. "I am trying these out for the fall menu."

"Mmmm …" Molly moaned as she bit off a big chunk from one. "These are delicious. I love the cinnamon, and is that ginger I taste?"

Star and Betty Sue added their compliments.

"Who's the sixth one for?" Betty Sue asked.

Her face fell as soon as she asked the question. The mood around the table changed instantly.

Just then, a commotion broke out on the beach.

"What's going on there?" Betty Sue boomed.

The Magnolias lined the deck and watched the drama unfolding on the beach.

Two men faced each other. Both of them held an aggressive stance.

"That's Peter Wilson," Jenny said with a gasp.

"Who's that ruffian standing before him?" Star asked. "Never seen him before."

Jenny peered at the unkempt man wearing an oversized coat. His face was smudged with dirt or soot and his hair was in total disarray.

"That looks like Mason," Jenny said.

"And who is that?" Betty Sue demanded.

"How do you know him?" Heather wasn't far behind.

"I don't, really. He's just a guy who hangs out on the beach."

"Hush, girls," Molly interrupted. "Can you hear what they are saying?"

Peter Wilson was waving his hands in the air, clearly disturbed about something. He jabbed a finger in the other man's chest and pushed him. Mason pushed Wilson back.

A crowd had begun to gather. People stood in a circle a few feet away from the two men, watching them intently.

Suddenly, Mason pulled something out of his coat pocket. It glinted in the sunlight.

"Oh my God, is that a gun?" Heather shrieked.

The Magnolias huddled together, struck speechless.

Peter Wilson took a step back. Mason held the gun in both hands and pointed it at Peter Wilson's chest. The crowd had begun to step back. Mason whirled around and pointed the gun to his right. A woman in the crowd grabbed her child and clutched him tightly.

Mason threw back his head and laughed. Every eye on the beach was trained on him now. He turned around again and pointed the gun at someone else.

"Let's go inside," Star said under her breath. "Start walking back very, very slowly. Do you hear me, girls? Don't make any sudden movements."

For once, Heather listened without any arguments and started inching back inside.

"Wait," Molly said. "That Wilson guy's saying something."

They saw Mason give a nod and put the gun back in his coat. He began walking away. The crowd parted to let him pass.

A few minutes later, Mason was out of sight.

"I think he's gone," Molly said.

Betty Sue had collapsed in her chair. Her brow was drenched in sweat. Jenny felt some beads of sweat on her own lip. They had almost been in the line of fire. Anything could have happened if the man had started shooting.

"What was that?" Star asked, sitting down with a thump.

No one spoke a word.

"That man is your friend?" Betty Sue thundered. "You need to be more careful, girl."

"He's not my friend," Jenny argued. "I've just seen him on the beach here. He walks around, scribbling something in the sand. I thought he might be hard up so I offered him a meal."

"I advise you to stay away from that man," Star said strongly. "You need to be more circumspect, Jenny."

"Shouldn't we report this?" Molly asked.

"Of course," Jenny agreed. "I'm calling Adam now."

She went into the kitchen and called the police station.

"Jenny!" His voice was laced with urgency and a good amount of fear. "Are you alright? All of you? I hear someone just pulled a gun on the beach."

"We are fine," Jenny assured him. "I was just calling to report that."

"We got multiple reports," Adam told her. "Some people even came in and demanded action."

"Are you going to arrest that man?"

"We'll bring him in for questioning. But I'm guessing he's long gone."

Jenny told him everything she knew about the man.

"Stay away from him in the future," Adam warned.

Jenny went back out. The Magnolias had calmed down a bit. A few groups of people came into the café and Jenny was kept busy for the next hour. Heather helped her serve the customers.

"Sit down," Star said when Jenny went out to the deck again.

"I don't agree with them," Molly said.

"What are you talking about?"

"Getting a gun," Betty Sue said. "You saw what just happened. You need to get a gun to protect yourself."

"I don't believe in guns," Jenny said flatly. "I'm surprised you are saying this, Betty Sue."

"My grandpa taught me how to shoot when I was eight," Betty Sue said. "I went hunting with him when I grew up. There was a rifle up on the wall in our living room, ready to greet any intruders."

"So what? We should all whip out our guns and shoot at each other?" Jenny asked, incensed.

"The town's changing," Star said. "We have more transients than we ever had before. There's nothing wrong in being prepared."

Jenny said nothing. Her aunt had a point.

"Look what happened to Barb Norton," Betty Sue continued.

"She had a close call," Star reminded Jenny.

"Did we find out who attacked her?" Heather asked. "I still think it was because of those ridiculous fines she imposed."

"She's not completely wrong," Betty Sue said grudgingly. "Mosquitoes and pests carry deadly diseases. We had a really bad outbreak one year, back in the 70s. It was the Rocky Mountain Spotted Fever. People died because of it."

"West Nile and Zika are bad too," Jenny noted. "Surely the people understand that? Barb might be a bit overzealous sometimes, but it's all for a good cause."

"Why did someone bash her on the head then?" Heather demanded.

"Do you think it was a prank?" Molly asked. "Kids from the high school having some fun?"

"Barb is too well known around town," Star said. "She probably knows most of the kids and their parents."

"How is Barb doing?" Jenny asked. "Has she recovered from the shock?"

"Today's the last day to pay the fines," Heather said. "And there's another meeting at the town hall tomorrow. Barb will be there alright, ready to pounce on people who haven't paid up."

The Magnolias dispersed soon after. Jenny was making chicken parmesan sandwiches for lunch. She stirred her homemade tomato sauce and seasoned it the way Petunia had taught her to. Heather had brought some fresh oregano and thyme from the inn's garden.

Vinny and his boys arrived and went to sit out on the deck. Jenny placed steaming sandwiches before them, smothered in melted mozzarella.

"How you doing, sweetheart?" Vinny asked her. "I heard someone pulled a gun out there today?"

Jenny assured him she was fine.

"You want me to set you up with a piece?" he asked.

"A piece of what?" Jenny asked, bewildered.

Smiley, Six Pac and Biggie burst out laughing.

"Never mind," Vinny said. "Someone comes bugging you, you let Vinny know. Alright, sweetheart?"

Jenny hoped Vinny was just grandstanding. She didn't want to think about the alternative. She pasted a smile on her face and served them big slices of chocolate cake.

Enzo Bellini arrived a few minutes after Vinny left. He was dressed in a blue tracksuit. He wore his signature fedora and chewed on his cigar.

"Fabio came to see me," he said to Jenny.

Jenny needed a few seconds to remember Fabio was none other than Peter Wilson.

"Who's this punk with a gun, anyway?" Enzo whispered. "I told Fabio to keep an eye on you."

"That's not necessary," Jenny protested.

"He's always taken care of the café. I don't see why that should stop now."

"Petunia ..." Jenny stuttered.

"My girl thought a lot about you," Enzo wheezed. "You are family now. And Enzo Bellini takes care of his own."

"Thanks," Jenny said shakily.

She wasn't sure what the old man expected from her.

Back home, Jenny spent the evening in her garden, admiring her roses as the sun went down over the horizon.

Dinner was a lively meal, with Jimmy and Star talking about a trip they wanted to take.

"Weren't you planning a trip to the mountains?" Star asked her.

"That was last year," Jenny said. "We never made it there. Adam hasn't said anything about a trip this year."

"Maybe we should all go together," Jimmy suggested.

"Talk to Adam about it," Star whispered, giving him a nudge.

Jenny rolled her eyes and ignored them. She was feeling stuffed after a lavish meal of crab cakes and oven baked fish. But she forced herself to lace up her walking shoes and go out for her walk.

Tank came bounding up after she had barely taken a few steps. She hugged him tight and pulled a battered tennis ball out of her pocket. She flung it in a wide arc, smiling as Tank leapt after it.

She finally looked up and met Adam's gaze.

"What a day, huh?" he breathed. "I'm so glad to see you are fine."

"Apparently, there's more than one person looking out for me."

"What does that mean?" Adam asked.

Jenny laughed and told him about Enzo's offer. Adam swore under his breath.

"You're getting a bit too close to these people."

"That's not all," Jenny said. "Betty Sue wants me to keep a gun at the café."

"No, no, Jenny." Adam shook his head vehemently. "That's not a good idea."

"Relax," Jenny cooed, taking his hand in hers. "I have already told them I am against the concept. I don't believe in violence."

"It's real," Adam said seriously. "But the café is full of civilians most of the time, including kids. Not a good place for guns."

"I know you can protect me, Adam," Jenny said. "The police station is less than a block away."

"Speaking of … who do you think has a license for an automatic?"

Jenny quirked an eyebrow and waited for Adam to continue.

"Laura Bellini, the teacher's wife."

"What does she want a gun for?"

"I'm going to find out," Adam said grimly. "I'm meeting her tomorrow to talk about it."

"Does she carry it around?"

"We don't know where the gun is. The local police in California are looking for it now."

"Can you prove she brought it to Pelican Cove the last time she was here?"

"We need to find the gun first. Once we have it, we can run all kinds of tests on it. We'll know if it was fired, for example."

"Do you think it's going to be that simple?" Jenny asked.

Her gut told her Laura Bellini was not a killer.

Chapter 13

Jenny was having lunch with Adam at the police station.

"I'm stuck, Adam," Jenny sighed. "I'm hitting a wall wherever I look."

Adam speared some more pasta salad on his fork and heard Jenny out. But he said nothing.

"How many people have you talked to?" he finally asked.

"I talked to people close to Petunia," Jenny said, counting off her fingers. "I am still not sure about Peter Wilson. But he has no motive and he also has the strongest alibi."

Jenny paused to take a bite of her chicken sandwich. Adam hadn't scowled or barked at her since she came in. She hoped his good mood would prevail. She had crossed her fingers behind her back and proceeded to pump him for information.

"The same applies to her sons, Vinny and Charles. They have alibis and no possible motive."

Jenny frowned as she pulled the lid off her salad container.

"I don't trust Laura Bellini though."

"Who else?" Adam asked.

"Actually, there is no one else. I'm going around in circles, evaluating the same people. I feel I am missing something. What about that man in the jacket?"

"We haven't made much progress with that," Adam said evasively.

He wolfed down the last piece of his sandwich and wiped his mouth with a paper napkin. He was looking forward to eating the apple pie Jenny had brought along. She had baked it with the first apples of the season.

"Why don't you let me talk to those people? They might remember something more."

"Sure. They hid the real story from us. They are just waiting for you to come along, right?"

"Don't be sarcastic, Adam. What do you have to lose?"

In Jenny's experience, people were naturally intimidated while talking to the police. She encouraged them to talk about anything, often ending up with relevant information which everyone had missed.

"I'm willing to try anything at this stage," Adam said, sounding dejected.

He wrote a few names on a notepad and tore the paper off, handing it to Jenny. He had added notes about where Jenny would find them.

Jenny went to the seafood market to shop for dinner. Chris Williams was nowhere to be seen. She realized Chris and Molly had their doctor's appointment that day. Her face broke into a smile. A baby would bring new life with it. Jenny looked forward to being an aunt.

"Do you remember the first time you met her?" Jenny asked Star that evening.

They sat out on the patio at Seaview, sipping wine before dinner. Roses and gardenias perfumed the air, their scent mingling with the salty breeze coming off the ocean.

Star had a faraway look in her eyes.

"It was on that rocky beach on the south side of town. I had set up my easel there to paint a commission. It was a cold, windy day. The wind caught one of my rags and I ran after it. Petunia was sitting behind a rock, staring out at the sea."

"Was she crying?"

Star thought a bit and shook her head.

"I think she was sad though. I asked her if she was new in town. She told me she needed a fresh start in life. I told her she had come to the perfect place."

"What did you do then?"

"I invited her home for coffee. She said she needed to keep busy. I told her how the town needed a decent diner."

"Was the café closed at that time?"

Star nodded.

"The previous owner, Millie, had died two years ago. Her son tried to run it for some time after that but he couldn't handle it. The café had been shut up since then."

"So she just bought the café?"

"She must have," Star said fondly. "The next thing I know, Petunia is serving coffee and making soup. She asked me to think of a name for the café because it had been my idea."

"And you thought of naming it the Boardwalk Café?"

"They were just building the new boardwalk at the time. It was supposed to be a big draw for the tourists. I thought Boardwalk Café sounded better than Millie's. Millie was gone anyway. Petunia loved the name. I painted the first sign for the café, you know."

"And you have been friends ever since?" Jenny asked, suddenly missing the warm, motherly woman who had never doubted her.

"We started meeting for coffee every morning," Star said wistfully. "Betty Sue asked if she could join us. Heather had just come to live with her. In a way, she was starting a new life, just like Petunia."

Jenny wondered if she would still be that close to Molly and Heather twenty five years later. At least she hoped to be.

"Petunia wasn't just my friend," Star said, her eyes welling with tears. "She was my sister. You need to find out who killed her, Jenny."

Jenny rubbed Star's arm, her gaze hardening with resolve.

"I'm doing everything I can," she promised. "How would you like to join me tomorrow? I am talking to a few people who might have seen something."

"Count me in," Star said.

They went in for dinner, leaning on each other.

Jenny sat out on the deck of the Boardwalk Café the next morning. She had asked Heather to come in and help her with breakfast. She had already baked a few batches of muffins and made crab salad for lunch.

"I need to talk to a couple of people today," she explained. "I'm hoping they will have some information for me."

Star sat next to Jenny, drawing something in her sketch pad. A woman came into view, walking a golden retriever. Jenny recognized her.

"Hello there," she waved.

The woman smiled uncertainly, pulling at the dog's leash to make him stop.

Jenny skipped down the café steps and ran the few steps to the woman.

"Can we talk? Please?"

"Sure," the woman shrugged. "Haven't I talked to you before?"

Jenny invited her to sit on the deck. She offered her some coffee.

"No, thanks. I only drink green juice in the mornings."

Star knew the woman well. They talked about a book club they both belonged to. The woman seemed to forget her hesitation after that.

"So what can I help you with?"

"It's about Petunia," Jenny began. "I hear you saw someone wearing a hooded jacket. Can we talk about that, please?"

The woman told Jenny what she already knew.

"Was there anything odd about that man? Anything that might have stood out?"

"All I remember is there was some kind of drawing on the back of that jacket. It was a bit frightening."

"Can you describe it?" Star said. "Let's see if I can come up with a sketch."

The woman's memory wasn't very clear. Star encouraged her to share any tiny detail she could think of. Star's fingers flew over her sketch pad as the woman talked. Finally, Star held up her pad.

"Was it something like this?"

Jenny's face crumpled when she saw what Star had drummed up. The picture didn't make any sense at all. The bottom part of it looked like a face or a skull. Feathers stuck out of the top, making it look like a bird of sorts.

The woman shook her head when she saw the drawing.

"That's not it." She shook her head. "Except for the

feathers. You got that part right."

"Was it a bird of some kind?" Jenny asked.

"I just remember the feathers," the woman repeated.

Her dog began barking his head off.

"I need to go," she said apologetically. "I'm here almost every morning in case you had more questions."

Jenny thanked her for her time and waved goodbye.

"This looks ridiculous!" Star groaned as she stared at the picture.

"We have one more person to talk to," Jenny said. "Let's go."

Jenny started her car and drove down half a mile to a gas station. A kid was working at the counter. He looked barely out of school. Jenny guessed he was eighteen or nineteen.

"I have a break coming up," the kid told them. "Can you wait until then?"

Jenny and Star sat in Jenny's car, fiddling with the radio until the kid came out. His name was Skinner and he was a high school dropout.

Skinner admitted he had noticed a man loitering around. He hadn't seen his face clearly because of the hooded jacket.

"You said there was some kind of picture on the back of the jacket?" Jenny asked hopefully. "Can you tell us about it?"

"It was weird, dude. Like a turkey coming to get ya."

"Can you describe it?" Star asked, pulling out a sketch pad. "I'm going to try and draw it."

Star's picture turned out to be a bird which looked very much like a turkey.

"You got the feathers right," the kid said. "There was something else. Like pirate stuff."

"You mean a skull?" Jenny asked eagerly.

"What's that funny hat Captain Sparrow wears?"

"A tricorn?"

Skinner shook his head.

"I don't know, dude. It wasn't anything I had seen before."

Jenny knew when she was beaten. She thanked the kid and drove back to the café.

"That was a waste of time," Star grumbled.

"They were both sure about the feathers."

"That doesn't make sense at all, Jenny."

"I am going to do some research on that," Jenny said stoutly as they drove back to the cafe.

Jason came to pick up lunch.

"I'm going to the mainland for an appointment," he told Jenny. "Can I get you something?"

Jenny shook her head absent mindedly.

"How about some Chinese food from your favorite place in town?" Jason smiled. "Looks like you're in a funk."

"I'm stumped," Jenny admitted. "And Chinese takeout sounds perfect for dinner. I'll bake some brownies for dessert."

"Now you're talking," Jason said, giving her a high five. "Don't worry, Jenny. We'll talk about it when I get back. Can you hold the fort down until then?"

Jenny nodded. She always felt better after talking to Jason.

They made short work of the takeout Jason brought

home. Jenny warmed the brownies and scooped generous portions of vanilla ice cream to go with them. She poured her special hot fudge on top and added a handful of chopped hazelnuts.

"I might have to run an extra mile tomorrow," Jason said, "but I'm digging into this tonight."

"Did you see those?" Jenny asked, pointing to the drawings Jason had been looking at. "Do they make any sense to you?"

"What are they?"

Jenny brought him up to speed.

"My guess is it could be a logo of some kind."

"I thought that too," Jenny said. "But who puts a skull on a logo? A tattoo parlor? A biker gang?"

"A gang!" they both cried together.

"Dial back a bit," Jenny exhaled. "What are you really saying, Jason?"

"I think we are getting ahead of ourselves," he said. "Have you looked this up online?"

"Not yet. I was planning to do that after dinner."

"Let's do it, then."

Star and Jimmy decided to sit out on the patio. Jenny sat with Jason at the kitchen table, running searches on skulls and feathers.

Jason told her about some forums frequented by private investigators.

"They are pretty cool about sharing information. Why don't you give them a brief description of what Star came up with? Add that it could be some kind of logo."

Jenny registered herself on a couple of websites and posted her question.

"Now what?" she asked Jason.

"Now we wait," Jason said. "Do you want to watch a movie?"

Jenny wanted to watch Downton Abbey reruns. Jason readily agreed.

"You're the best, Jason!" Jenny exclaimed, giving him a hug. "What would I do without you?"

Jason hugged her back and planted a kiss on her forehead. He held her by the arms and stared deep into her eyes.

"If I have my way, Jenny King, you'll never have to find out."

Chapter 14

Jenny's laptop pinged just as the second episode of Downton Abbey came to an end. She got up eagerly to check it out.

"A guy in Atlanta believes it could be a gang logo," she told Jason.

"Can he be more specific?" Jason asked.

Jenny pursed her lips.

"That's all he says."

The computer pinged again.

"Oh wait. Someone else is writing a reply to my question. He calls himself TopNJPI."

Jason stifled a yawn.

"What does this one say?"

"He says the feathers sound familiar. He wants me to send him a picture."

"Do it."

Jenny looked around for Star's drawings. She had shoved them in a kitchen drawer. She clicked a photo with her phone and sent it on.

Jason came and sat next to Jenny. They waited impatiently for the man to respond.

Jenny read his reply off the screen.

"He says the feathers make him think of a local Jersey gang."

"A biker gang?" Jason asked quizzically. "Is this guy sure?"

Jenny typed furiously, talking with a man she had never met or heard of before.

"He is asking me to look up the Purple Rooster gang."

Jason pulled out his phone and started typing. Jenny did the same with her computer. They looked at each other at the same time.

Jason showed her the picture he had pulled up on his phone.

"It does look a bit like Star's drawing," Jenny said grudgingly. "But it's not the same."

"Nothing matches other than the feathers," Jason said.

Jenny started pulling up information on the Purple Rooster gang.

"Oh my!" she exclaimed as her mouth fell open. "The Purple Rooster is a street gang in New Jersey."

"What do they do?"

"They are involved in all kinds of illegal activities, mostly drugs. But that's not all, Jason."

"Get on with it, Jenny."

"They are connected to some big crime family."

"That's not uncommon," Jason said.

"This family is supposedly at war with the Bellinis."

Jenny and Jason were both speechless.

"You don't think this gang came here to kill Petunia?" Jenny asked haltingly. "She walked away from that life a long time ago."

"But she was still a Bellini," Jason said softly.

He tapped his fingers on the table.

"This is too big for you or me, Jenny. You need to take this to the police."

"What about Vinny? Shouldn't I tell him first?"

"There's no telling how he will react to this," Jason warned.

"This is all speculative," Jenny argued. "I think we should talk to Vinny first."

"Do you have his number?"

Jenny nodded.

Vinny offered to meet her somewhere. Jenny reluctantly invited him to Seaview.

"Do you know what you're doing?" Star asked.

"I'm doing it for Petunia," Jenny said.

Vinny arrived with Enzo in tow. Enzo was wearing another track suit. Vinny was dressed in a cream colored suit tailored to perfection. Both men wore white colored fedoras. Six Pac and the guys stayed outside with the car.

Jenny didn't waste any time in showing Vinny the drawings.

"What's this, sweetheart?" Vinny asked, chewing on his cigar. "Some kind of art project?"

Jenny told them about the man in the hooded jacket.

"I did some digging. I think he was from the Purple Rooster gang."

Vinny and Enzo both threw back their heads and

laughed.

"What do you know about the Purple Roosters?"

"Nothing," Jenny admitted. "But I thought this picture looked like their logo."

"The feathers are a bit familiar," Vinny conceded. "But they are not purple."

"Aren't you fighting with that gang?" Jenny asked.

Vinny and Enzo looked at each other.

"Not anymore," Enzo said. "I had a beef with those boys thirty years ago. But I made up with them when I was in prison."

"Wait. Are you thinking the Purple Roosters whacked my Ma?" Vinny asked.

Jenny was beginning to feel embarrassed.

"It was just a thought. I have no other suspects."

"They wouldn't dare put a hit on my girl," Enzo whispered. "But since you brought it up, I am going to ask around."

"Did many people know Petunia was living in Pelican Cove?"

"Most people thought she was dead," Enzo whispered.

"I let them think that. It was easier than answering questions about what happened to her."

"Do you think Peter Wilson, err Fabio, could have told anyone about Petunia?"

Enzo looked at her coldly.

"My men are loyal to me, girl. I trust Fabio with my life. I trusted him with my baby girl's life. He took care of her all these years."

Vinny and Enzo ate Jenny's brownies before they went back.

"What do you think, Jason?" Jenny asked. "Was someone taking care of an old grudge?"

"Why wait so long to do that? Petunia lived here without incident for twenty five years."

Something Enzo had said niggled at Jenny.

"What if this person was unable to track her down?"

"You mean what if he or she was in prison."

"Is that too farfetched?" Jenny frowned.

"It does seem fantastic at first." Jason narrowed his eyes. "But it's not farfetched, Jenny. I have heard of stranger things in court."

"How did this person find Petunia? She hadn't talked to any of her family members since she came here."

"Peter Wilson!" they both exclaimed together.

"He was her only link to her old life," Jenny said in triumph. "His alibi doesn't help him here. What if Peter Wilson told someone about Petunia?"

"I think you might have something there, Jenny," Jason nodded. "But this is bigger than you can handle."

"I will go to the police station first thing tomorrow morning," Jenny promised. "They can question Wilson about this."

Jenny went up to her room after bidding Jason goodnight. She hoped her latest theory would lead them to the killer. She was saddened by the thought of Petunia being the victim of some old feud. She tossed and turned under the covers, waiting impatiently for the sun to rise.

Star accompanied Jenny to the café the next morning. She wasn't used to early mornings. Jenny forced her to sit down and put her feet up after she had yawned nonstop for fifteen minutes.

Jenny poured her a fresh cup of coffee.

"You didn't have to come in with me. I have to learn

to handle everything myself."

"This work is too much for one person," Star argued as Jenny mixed the muffin batter. "You can't work in the kitchen and serve the customers at the same time."

"What if I ask them to serve themselves?" Jenny thought out loud. "I can just set everything out on a couple of tables."

"You need to think seriously about hiring some help, Jenny."

"I know that," Jenny said. "Just not yet."

Adam came in for breakfast.

"We have a lot to talk about," Jenny told him as she served him the breakfast special, a three cheese omelet with spinach and sundried tomatoes.

"You want to talk here?" Adam asked.

"No. Let me take care of the breakfast rush. I'll see you at the station."

Heather came in to help. Jenny packed some fresh oatmeal raisin cookies in a box and walked to the police station. She handed the box to Nora, the desk clerk.

"Just what I needed," Nora said happily.

"No cookies for me?" Adam teased when she entered his office.

"Too much sugar is not good for you," Jenny kidded.

She told Adam about the gang logo first.

"The Purple Rooster gang used to be notorious," Adam told her. "But they have fizzled out in the past few years. Their leader was killed and most of the older members went to prison."

"So you don't think they could have a hand in this?"

"The Bellinis don't think so, do they?"

Jenny shook her head.

"Can you double check, just in case?"

"This is out of my jurisdiction, Jenny. But I'll put some feelers out."

Jenny continued her theory about old feuds.

Adam's eyebrows shot up.

"That's one line of investigation we haven't pursued."

"Do you think there's any substance to it, though?"

"If it was a gang hit, we may never find out who did it, Jenny."

Adam had turned serious.

"We are hitting a wall wherever we turn," Jenny said in frustration.

"I know your efforts helped us solve some murders, Jenny. But things don't often work that way."

Jenny turned to Peter Wilson.

"He was the only one who knew Petunia's real identity," Jenny stressed. "He has to be involved in this somehow."

"These fellows are generally pretty loyal," Adam mused. "I don't see Wilson going against his boss. He has his own family to think about."

"That's all I have," Jenny sighed. "But none of this helps."

"We are doing all we can, Jenny. Don't give up yet."

"Have you checked Laura Bellini's finances?" Jenny asked suddenly.

She told Adam about the million dollars Petunia had given her.

"There's something else about Laura," Adam said reluctantly. "Police didn't find the gun registered to her."

"You think she ditched it?"

"She said it went missing."

"She has to be lying, Adam."

"Laura said she reported her missing gun long before coming to Pelican Cove."

"The first time or the second time?"

Adam was apologetic.

"We are still following up on that."

Adam's phone rang. Jenny caught a few random words as the person on the other end let loose a tirade. Adam apologized repeatedly. Jenny stared at him in amazement. She had never seen him so subdued before.

Adam hung up the phone and rubbed his eyes with his hands.

"That was Barb," he sighed. "She's not happy."

"How is she?" Jenny asked with genuine concern.

"Recovering nicely, judging by her energy."

Barb Norton was well known for making absurd demands of everyone. But Jenny knew she was justified this time.

"She wants to know why we haven't caught her attacker yet," Adam disclosed.

"Why haven't you?"

"We don't have a single eyewitness," Adam growled, frustrated. "It's almost like some phantom figure hit her and disappeared in thin air."

"Just like Petunia," Jenny said softly.

She sat straighter, her eyes growing wide as a sudden thought hit her.

"What if the two incidents are related? Could someone be targeting older women?"

"I don't think so, Jenny," Adam dismissed.

"Why not?" Jenny argued. "They were both the same age. They were both the same height and build although Petunia's hair was darker."

"Stop right there, Jenny," Adam warned. "I have too many things to work on already. I don't want you to start a panic in town with these silly theories."

"It's not silly," Jenny said coldly. "I think it's worth thinking about. It's not like you have any tangible leads, anyway."

"I can't stop you, Jenny. Do what you want."

"Let's not fight, please," Jenny urged.

Adam's voice turned softer.

"That's the last thing I want to do, Jenny."

"Why don't you come to Seaview for dinner tonight?" Jenny wheedled. "I'm making enchiladas. Bring Tank with you."

"Sounds like a plan," Adam smiled. "We'll get dessert."

"Are the twins coming here for fall break?"

"Probably," Adam said. "I plan to make it worth their while."

"Planning something special?" Jenny asked.

Adam hid a smile but said nothing.

Jenny set a brisk pace back to the café, enjoying the pleasant weather. She decided it was a good time to call her son.

"When are you coming home, Nicky?"

"Looks tough, Mom," her son said, breaking into a coughing fit. "I have too many classes this time."

Jenny knew her son always started coughing when he was lying. She wondered what he was hiding this time.

"Are you and the twins stirring up trouble?" she asked suspiciously.

Her son and Adam's twins went to different colleges but they talked to each other regularly.

"Of course not, Mother," Nick said, starting to cough again.

Jenny smiled all the way back to the café. She could be patient when needed. She guessed Adam had a surprise for her. Maybe there was still some hope for them.

Chapter 15

A crisp breeze blew over the ocean the next morning, signaling the arrival of fall. On the deck of the Boardwalk Café, the Magnolias stared with amazement at Molly, their coffee forgotten.

"What do you mean, you were mistaken?" Heather cried. "How is that possible?"

Molly blushed.

"You know …"

"How did you find out?" Jenny asked gently, placing a hand on Heather to calm her down.

"At the doctor's," Molly said. "It was so embarrassing."

"Was Chris with you?" Heather asked.

Molly nodded.

Betty Sue leaned forward in her chair, her knitting needles clacking in a fast rhythm.

"You do know how these things are supposed to happen?" she asked Molly.

Molly looked like she was about to burst into tears.

"Begin at the beginning," Star ordered. "I think I am missing something here."

"It's all pretty straightforward," Molly shrugged. "Chris and I went to our doctor's appointment. It was my first appointment for the baby. Turns out I am not pregnant. I never was."

All the women at the table looked sorry.

"I was knitting this for the baby," Betty Sue said, holding up something fluffy in a peach color.

"How did Chris take it?" Jenny asked.

"He was disappointed. So was I."

"What now?" Star wanted to know.

"This whole misunderstanding forced us to consider parenthood," Molly admitted. "I was very impressed by how Chris reacted to it."

"Chris Williams is a good man," Betty Sue sighed.

For the past twenty years or so, she had believed he would marry her granddaughter Heather.

Jenny knew Molly hadn't been very sure about how committed Chris was to her.

"Do you trust him now?" she asked Molly.

"I trust him more," Molly said diplomatically. "I know he is going to be a good father."

"So when are you planning a family?" Star laughed. "For real, this time."

Molly blushed prettily.

"Soon."

"Let them get married first," Jenny nudged her aunt. "Have you thought about setting a date?"

Earlier that year, Chris and Molly had started wearing promise rings.

"Don't you want a proper engagement first?" Star asked.

"We are talking about it," Molly told them.

"I think you should just elope." Heather winked.

"No, thanks!" Molly said firmly. "This might be my second wedding, but I want to do it right."

Jenny secretly looked forward to planning Molly's wedding. She had come to love Molly like a sister, and she hoped to be in the wedding party.

Jenny spotted Vinny walking on the beach, accompanied by his posse. Molly followed her gaze.

"How's your search going, Jenny?" she asked.

"I have a lot of theories," Jenny admitted reluctantly. "But there is no proof to support any of them."

"You just haven't found it yet," Star said encouragingly. "Keep looking, sweetie."

"I almost forgot," Jenny exclaimed. "Jason and I are meeting Adam in a few minutes."

Jason stepped out on the patio just then. He greeted the Magnolias and looked inquiringly at Jenny.

"Ready to go?"

Jenny pulled off her apron and nodded. They went down the steps to the beach on their way to the police station.

"Do you think Adam will agree?"

Jenny was feeling doubtful about their mission.

"What does he have to lose?" Jason quipped.

Adam wasn't too happy to see them.

"I have a long day ahead of me, Jenny. What are you two doing here?"

"We have a request," Jason said. "We want access to the traffic cameras."

"Why?" Adam asked, tapping his pencil on the desk.

Jenny reminded Adam about the car in the parking lot.

"I am almost sure the killer escaped in that car. We need to find out where it went."

"The cameras might have caught the tag plates," Jason said hopefully. "Who knows? We may even get a glimpse of the driver."

"Okay," Adam said grudgingly. "I am only doing this because I need a break in the case. But you will have to watch the tapes here."

Jason and Jenny agreed readily.

"How are we going to do this?" Jenny asked.

One of the techs at the police station helped them. They decided to focus on the road around the parking lot. They chose a time slot of 5 to 8 AM, the approximate time of Petunia's death.

"We should watch for a dark sedan with a dent around the trunk."

It was slow work. Nora, the desk clerk, came around to chat with Jenny. Jenny made some polite conversation. They drank the sour coffee Nora offered. Jenny took one sip and set it aside.

"I don't see any cars matching the description," Jason said after some time.

He was beginning to look frustrated.

"Let's widen the search," Jenny suggested.

Jason was staring at one camera which showed a gas station.

"You think that guy might have gone in here?" he wondered.

They decided to look at all the cars going into the gas station. None of the cars stopping at the station matched the description of the car they were looking for.

"What's that kid doing there?" Jason asked, pointing at a figure. "He seems to be in and out of that door a lot."

"That must be Skinner," Jenny said. "He works at the gas station. He does a lot of odd jobs in addition to managing the cash register."

Jenny grew bored as the tapes rolled slowly. She yawned and that set Jason off.

"Hold it," Jenny cried suddenly.

She was pointing to something on the screen.

"What's that? That right there?"

Jason paused the picture and peered at the screen.

"Looks like the same kid."

"What is he wearing?" Jenny asked in a hushed voice.

"A jacket?"

"Look at the back of the jacket, Jason," Jenny said.

"Hmmm … looks like something's printed on the back."

Jenny made Jason zoom in to the picture. She could make out a few feathers.

"Wanna bet it's the same jacket?" Jenny banged a fist on the table. "That little creep. He lied to us."

"Hold it, Jenny. What are you blabbering about?"

Jenny explained her theory to Jason.

"Let's go talk to him," Jason said, leaping up.

Jenny's cell phone rang when Jason was driving to the gas station. It was Adam.

"What's going on? Where did you rush off all of a sudden?"

Jenny gave him the condensed version.

"Turn around right now!" Adam ordered. "You are not going there alone."

"Jason is here with me."

"You are both crazy. What if this kid is really the person we are looking for? He could have a gun."

"Relax!" Jenny said. "I've met that kid. He's harmless."

Adam became more incensed.

"You don't know that, Jenny. Please stop the car immediately. Let me talk to Jason."

"Jason says we can handle it."

"Stop right now, or I will arrest you both for messing with police business."

"Don't be such a grouch, Adam."

Jenny hung up the phone.

"What did he say?" Jason asked her.

"That's just Adam being Adam."

A police car with flashing lights and a blaring siren overtook them two minutes later. It pulled into the gas station's parking lot ahead of Jason. Adam stumbled out, leaning on his cane. He looked ready to burst.

"That was quick," Jenny said glibly.

"I'll deal with you later, Jenny." He turned toward Jason. "Let me do the talking."

"Fine by me," Jason shrugged.

The kid working at the gas station came out to see what was happening.

"This is Skinner," Jenny introduced him.

"Do you work here?" Adam asked.

The kid looked like he was about to bolt.

"I ain't done nothing wrong," he said sullenly.

"No one's saying you did," Adam snapped. "I need to ask you a few questions."

The kid shrugged.

"I got nothing to hide."

"You remember what we talked about?" she began. "You told us you didn't know the guy in the hoodie."

"So what?"

"We saw you wearing the same jacket later that day,"

Jenny said. "How did you get it if you didn't know that man?"

The kid's eyes filled with fear.

"I found it in the dumpster. I swear."

"You better not be lying, son," Adam said sternly.

"I'm not lying. I found it in the dumpster out back. It was a windy day and I was feeling cold. So I wore it."

"You picked it up from the trash?" Adam asked.

Skinner was defensive.

"I don't go dumpster diving. But there was nothing wrong with that jacket. Can't be too picky, you know. I don't even make minimum wage."

"I think he's telling the truth," Jenny said supportively.

"Thank you for your opinion," Adam said coldly. He turned toward Skinner. "We will need to look at your security cameras."

"You have to talk to my boss," the kid said. "But we don't have any cameras near the dumpster."

"Are you sure?" Adam asked.

"There's a camera out back but it's broken. The dumpster's out of its range anyway."

Adam asked a few more questions but he had to let the kid go.

He stalked back to his car and left without a word.

"Looks like he's really mad at you, Jenny."

Jason drove to Ethan's Crab Shack for lunch. Ethan was Adam's twin. He had the same imposing height and deep blue eyes but the similarities ended there. The deeply etched laugh lines around his face were a testament to his cheerful personality.

Ethan greeted her with a hug.

"Haven't seen you in a while, Jenny."

Jason ordered the special of the day, which was an assortment of fried fish and crabs. Ethan brought up a platter loaded with hand cut fries and hush puppies. Jenny couldn't wait to dip them into his special tartar sauce.

"I'm sorry I wasted your time."

"What are you talking about?" Jason acted surprised. "I had a wonderful day."

"We hit another wall," Jenny said gloomily.

"We did find something," Jason reminded her. "So far, we had only heard about that jacket. Now we know it did exist. That means the man is real too."

"You're right," Jenny said, cheering up.

"What happened to the car, though?" Jason mused. "That's a big puzzle."

Jenny bit off a piece of fried flounder. It melted in her mouth.

"I'm losing hope, Jason. I don't think we are ever going to find out the truth."

"Don't give up yet, Jenny. We just have to keep looking."

"How is that grumpy brother of mine behaving?" Ethan boomed as he set bowls of peach cobbler before them.

Jenny rolled her eyes.

"He just threw a fit. Would you believe it?"

"That's his way of showing his love," Ethan laughed.

Jenny felt her cheeks burn.

"Has he always been like this?"

"He's changed a lot since he met you, Jenny," Ethan assured her. "For the better."

Jenny thought of Ethan's words as she walked on the beach after dinner. A big hairy body almost toppled her.

"Tank! You adorable darling! I missed you."

She patted the big dog and scratched him under his ears. Tank butted her in the knee and sat down in the sand.

Adam stood in the shadows, looking at her with a guarded expression.

"I was hoping to run into you."

"Me too," Adam said, clearing his throat.

They walked for a while, Tank running in circles around them, wagging his tail.

Jenny wondered if Adam expected her to apologize.

"I am sorry, Jenny," he said suddenly.

He pulled her close to him and hugged her tightly.

"You scared the hell out of me."

"I'm fine, Adam. See?"

"What if that kid had pulled out a gun?"

"People in Pelican Cove don't own guns. You told me

so yourself."

"But someone does have a gun, Jenny. Someone who shot Petunia in cold blood."

"Thank you for worrying about me," Jenny said softly.

"Of course I worry," Adam said. "You are the light of my life, Jenny King. What would I do if anything happened to you?"

Chapter 16

The Magnolias were sitting out on the deck, having their mid-morning coffee break. The café had been unusually busy for breakfast and Jenny was exhausted.

"We ran out of muffins," she explained as she set out some cookies with the coffee. "Why don't you all stay on for lunch?"

"You have enough on your plate without us crowding you," Molly said. "I wish I could help you more, Jenny. But I can't get away from my desk at the library."

"Heather and Star are both pitching in," Jenny said gratefully. "I don't know what I would do without them."

"Petunia was a quiet one, wasn't she?" Star said.

"But she did the lion's share of work around here," Jenny spoke up. "She was always there, telling me what to do next. I need to make all those decisions now and I am not good at them."

"You will learn," Betty Sue consoled her. "What other option do you have?"

"Petunia always spoke up when it mattered," Molly pointed out. "She wasn't afraid to voice her opinion."

Jenny closed her eyes and leaned back in her chair.

"I miss her so much!"

"We all do, sweetie," Star said, stroking her back.

Barb Norton puffed up the steps of the Boardwalk Café, scratching her arm.

"How are you, Barb?" Betty Sue asked solicitously. "Have you recovered from that bump on your head?"

Barb assumed the air of a martyr.

"It's the price I pay for what I do."

Heather giggled.

"Stop tittering at my plight, young lady. Hasn't your grandma taught you better?"

"Leave my girl alone," Betty Sue snapped. "What do you want?"

"Did you get my letter about the fines?" Barb's tone was acerbic. "Hardly anyone has paid up."

"You can't penalize people just because they have some water in their bird feeders," Star scoffed. "Get real, Barb. No one is paying those ridiculous fines."

"How do you propose we deal with these mosquitoes then?" Barb asked, scratching her neck now.

Her arm and neck had both turned red.

"Stop scratching, Barb!" Betty Sue hollered. "You're making it worse."

"These little bloodsuckers keep biting me."

"They must like you a lot," Heather grinned.

Jenny took pity on the woman.

"Would you like a cookie, Barb?"

"I want more than one. How about five dozen?"

"Huh?" Jenny was bewildered.

"I am putting together a bake sale," Barb said. "It's the only way to raise money for the extermination."

"I'm sorry I can't help you this time."

"But I am counting on you, Jenny. Pelican Cove is counting on you."

"I'm up to my ears in work, Barb. Plus I still have to plan Petunia's memorial. There's no way I can squeeze this in."

"Petunia would never have turned her back on me," Barb said cagily.

"That's below the belt, Barb!" Star exclaimed.

"Take that back!" Betty Sue cried.

Heather and Molly watched on with their eyes wide.

Jenny caved.

"Two dozen cookies, Barb. That's it. Any kind I choose."

"That'll be just fine, dear," Barb smiled. "Don't forget the meeting tonight, girls. I will see you there."

"Does she ever get tired of these meetings?" Molly groaned.

"She just likes to boss people around," Star quipped.

"She was right about Petunia," Jenny sighed. "How can I ever live up to her?"

"You are doing good, kid," Star assured her. "She would be proud of you."

The other women agreed with Star. They tried to cheer Jenny up. She thought they were just being kind.

"Any luck watching those cameras?" Heather asked.

"We watched the traffic cams in town yesterday," Jenny told her. "Didn't find much."

"I admire your patience. You must have looked at every camera in town."

"What was that?" Jenny asked suddenly. "Heather, you are brilliant!"

She ran inside and called Jason.

"I just thought of something. What are you doing right now?"

Jason invited her to come over.

"Can you handle the lunch crowd again?" she asked her aunt. "Soup's almost done. I already mixed the chicken salad."

Star assured her she would be fine. Jenny hurried to Jason's office. She apologized for disturbing him.

"I don't have anything on my calendar," he assured her. "Just some paper work. You know I'll do anything to get out of that."

Jenny tried to curb her excitement.

"This might be nothing," she began. "But something Heather said got me thinking."

"Go on," Jason encouraged her.

"We looked at the tapes at the police station. But what about other cameras in town?"

"Didn't you already talk to some store owners? I

thought no one in Pelican Cove used security cameras."

"Those were places along the beach," Jenny nodded. "But there's another camera we can look at."

Jason looked blank.

"The gas station!" Jenny exclaimed. "Remember what that kid Skinner said about the camera at the back?"

"It wasn't working?"

"Right. But I'm sure they have more cameras around the front."

"That does seem logical," Jason said. "Want to go check them out?"

Jenny was relieved to find Skinner working at the gas station.

"We want to look at your security cameras."

"Weren't you here yesterday?" he asked sullenly. "I told you the camera at the back was busted."

"How many more cameras do you have?" Jason asked.

The kid shrugged.

"A few, I guess."

Jenny and Jason went out and walked around the little store. Jenny squinted in the bright noon sunshine, trying to spot the cameras.

They counted four more. Jenny pointed to a camera mounted near the entrance to the parking lot. The road directly led to the dumpster at the back.

"We don't need the dumpster camera," she said eagerly. "Our man would have to enter from somewhere right? Any of these cameras might have caught him."

Jason agreed with her theory. They went back inside.

"We want to look at your tapes."

"It's all set up in that little office at the back," he said. "I'm not allowed to go in there."

"Do you want me to call the Sheriff?" Jason asked. "He can come here with a warrant and seal your place."

"Take it easy, mister," the kid complained. "I don't want to lose my job."

He pulled his phone out of his pocket and tapped some keys. He thrust the phone in Jason's face.

"That's my boss. Why don't you call him and sort it out. Keep me out of it, okay?"

Jason started dialing the number.

"I didn't tell you about the cameras," Skinner reminded him.

Jason stepped outside and Jenny followed him.

The gas station owner turned out to be a guy Jason knew well. Jenny folded her hands and leaned against a wall, waiting for Jason to get on with it. Jason got to the point after five minutes of small talk.

"We went to high school together," Jason told Jenny when he hung up.

"Not hard to believe, considering you know everyone in town."

"He knows Adam too," Jason explained. "And he knew Petunia well."

"What about the cameras?" Jenny was getting impatient.

"He says we have full access. We can look at any footage we want. He's going to call the kid and let him know."

The phone rang inside just as Jenny pushed the door open. Skinner gave some brief replies and hung up.

"I'm supposed to let you in there," he grumbled.

He pulled out a big bunch of keys from a drawer and ambled to the back. A small door lay hidden behind stacks of merchandise. The kid tried a couple of keys before he found the right one.

"Can you figure this thing out?" he asked, pointing at a computer on a tiny desk. "Just holler if you want something."

Jenny was feeling parched.

"Actually, I could use some coffee."

"I can ring it up for you," Skinner nodded.

Jenny glanced at a half full flask sitting on a warmer and decided to pass. She filled two cups from an automatic coffee machine. It was sweeter than she preferred but at least it didn't taste bitter.

The office at the back was barely bigger than a closet. Jason pointed to the tiny chair. Jenny squeezed into it, hugging her knees together. Jason stood behind her with his back against the wall.

Jenny started the computer and waited for it to boot up. The desktop had a folder titled 'security footage'. She clicked on it to find a bunch of folders arranged by week. Each folder contained a file for a particular day.

"This looks well organized," Jason said.

They pulled up the file for the day in question. The picture was slightly grainy at first.

"That's before sunrise," Jason noted.

They skimmed through the whole tape without much luck.

"What exactly are we looking for?" Jason asked. "A dark colored sedan?"

"What if the man just walked in for a drink or something? He may have parked his car somewhere else."

"Run the video again, Jenny. We'll focus on the people this time."

Jenny's stomach growled.

"Oops," Jenny apologized. "I had a light breakfast today."

"Hold on," Jason said.

He went out into the store and came back a few minutes later, clutching a bunch of snacks. Jenny chose an energy bar and bit off a big chunk.

"Thanks."

Jason started munching on some potato chips.

They peered at the people entering and leaving the store. Jenny grew frustrated after an hour had passed.

"This is a big waste of time."

"We have looked at a couple dozen people," Jason agreed.

"None of them walked to the back of the store," Jenny noted. "I don't see how that jacket appeared in the dumpster. Unless it was there all along?"

"That's not possible," Jason pointed out. "Our man was seen wearing it that morning, remember?"

Jenny suddenly jabbed her finger at the screen.

"What's that?"

A disheveled man was pushing a shopping cart ahead of him. It was filled with some boxes and knick knacks. A dark colored cloth lay on top.

"Can you zoom in on that?" Jason asked.

Jenny fiddled with the mouse and enlarged the portion showing the cart.

"Do you see those feathers?" Jenny exclaimed. "That's our jacket."

"What's it doing in that cart?"

"Do you know who that man is?" Jenny asked Jason.

"Looks like a hobo, Jenny, or someone down on his luck."

Jenny reversed and forwarded the video, training her eyes on the man with the cart. He came out of the store carrying something wrapped in paper. He wheeled his cart to one end of the parking lot and sat down.

"That looks like a hot dog," Jenny said, as the man on the screen unwrapped the object he was carrying.

He ate the hot dog very slowly, as if savoring each bite. Then he just sat on the ground, staring into the distance.

A figure came out from the store and walked toward the man with the cart.

"That's the kid," Jason said, stamping his foot to get some circulation going.

Their mouths dropped open as they watched the screen.

"I don't believe it!" Jenny yelled. "That little creep!"

Jenny and Jason rushed outside to the cash register. Skinner was packing some stuff into a backpack.

"Where do you think you're going?" Jenny cried.

Skinner looked up with a pained expression.

"Home? My shift's over."

He nodded at a young girl who was coming in.

"You lied to us," Jason said sternly.

"You didn't find the jacket in the dumpster," Jenny seethed.

"Okay, okay, calm down. I took it from some guy."

"Do you realize this is a murder investigation?" Jason fumed. "I could have you arrested for obstruction."

"I don't want no trouble," Skinner said, holding up his hands. "I liked the jacket so I took it."

"Do you know where the man got it?"

"No idea. I just took it and he didn't say a word."

"Did you see where he went?" Jenny asked.

"Sorry," Skinner said, shaking his head. "Never saw him again."

"Would you recognize him if you saw him?" Jason asked.

"I don't think so. I didn't really look at him."

Chapter 17

That evening, Jenny sat alone in the Rusty Anchor, Pelican Cove's one and only pub. She was waiting for Adam. She saw a lot of familiar faces around her and waved at a couple of them. But she didn't get up and go talk to anyone.

Eddie Cotton, the bartender and pub owner, placed a glass of wine before her.

"What's got into you, Jenny? You seem quiet."

Jenny's eyes filled up.

"I'm trying everything I can to find Petunia's killer. But I can't seem to catch a break."

"If anyone can do it, Jenny, you can," Eddie said loyally.

Jenny thanked him for his kindness. Adam finally entered the pub. He was out of uniform.

"Sorry I'm late," he said, taking a seat. "I wanted to go home and change."

They were going out to dinner after drinks.

"Where do you want to eat, Jenny?" Adam asked

solicitously.

"I don't care," Jenny said. "We can pick up a pie at Mama Rosa's and go home."

"Are you still thinking about that jacket?" Adam asked.

Jenny and Jason had gone to meet Adam from the gas station. He had been impressed by what they had discovered. He was going to look for the man with the shopping cart.

"My men are scouring the nearby towns for that man," Adam assured her. "We tried to get his picture off that video."

"It's probably another dead end," Jenny said darkly.

"Don't lose hope yet, Jenny," Adam comforted her. "We'll get there."

Jenny didn't have the heart to face Vinny the next day. He came to the café twice every day. He greeted Jenny and asked after her. He relished whatever food she put before him. He didn't say much but Jenny found his silence suffocating. She felt he was waiting for her to work her magic and catch the killer.

Star and Betty Sue, the older Magnolias, sat out on the deck. Betty Sue was busy knitting something with lavender yarn.

"What about Barb's grandson?" Star asked.

"The one in Florida?" Betty Sue scoffed. "He's barely out of school."

"Not that one," Star said. "I mean her niece's son. He used to spend his summers in town."

"The one who wears those fancy suits and works in New York?" Betty Sue asked, her eyes gleaming. "He might work. Do you know how old he is?"

"He must be thirty at least," Star said.

"That's younger than my Heather."

"Age doesn't matter anymore," Star quipped. "I think these modern girls prefer younger boys."

Betty Sue puffed up in protest.

"What is the world coming to? That wasn't how it was in my day. Beaus were a lot older than girls. They had to be."

"What are you two up to?" Jenny asked, bringing out a fresh pot of coffee.

Molly had some extra work at the library and she couldn't get away for a break.

"We are just talking," Star said, clamming up. "The

usual gossip, you know."

"Where's Heather?"

"Heather's out walking Tootsie," Betty Sue said. "She should be here any minute."

Tootsie was the Morse family poodle and was heavily pampered by Heather and Betty Sue.

"So you're talking about Heather," Jenny winked.

"Betty Sue's trying to set her up with a suitable boy," Star burst out.

Betty Sue muttered under her breath.

"Heather wants to focus on the inn," Jenny told them. "She doesn't have time for men."

"That's what worries me," Betty Sue nodded. "She's almost thirty five. Is she ever going to settle down?"

"All in good time," Star shrugged.

"I don't get it, Betty Sue," Jenny protested. "Just a few weeks ago, you were worried Heather was going out with the wrong kind of men. Now that she's finally sworn off them, you want her to start dating again?"

"I want her to date the right kind of man," Betty Sue cried.

"Someone like Chris, you mean?" Jenny smirked.

"Better than him," Betty Sue said. "Heather's pretty and smart. She runs a business almost singlehandedly. She needs a man who can recognize and respect her abilities."

"I agree with that," Jenny nodded. "But where is she going to find someone like that in Pelican Cove?"

"Who are you talking about?" a voice spoke in Jenny's ear, making her jump.

"Heather!" Jenny exclaimed. "When did you get here? And where's Tootsie?"

"Back home playing with her toys. What are you ladies up to?"

"You're late, Heather!" Betty Sue complained. "It's time to get back to the inn."

"Actually, Heather," Jenny said. "How about a drive?"

"You know I'm your wing woman," Heather grinned. "Just point the way, Captain."

Jenny looked inquiringly at her aunt.

"Go," Star said. "I got the café covered."

"Lunch is ready," Jenny promised. "And I won't be

long."

Jenny drove toward the gas station.

"What's the plan?" Heather asked.

"It's a bit silly," Jenny admitted. "I am hoping to run into that man with the cart."

"You think he might be at the gas station again," Heather deduced. "Fingers crossed, then. You never know."

Jenny parked her car and cracked a window open. Heather got out to get some snacks. Skinner came out of the store and waved at Jenny.

Heather and Jenny worked through two big packets of fried, salty stuff and guzzled sodas.

"I have to go in," Jenny said.

"I've been keeping an eye out for him," Skinner told her. "I know how badly you want to talk to him."

Jenny gave up some time later and drove back to the café. She dropped Heather off at the Bayview Inn first.

"Adam rang for you," Star told her just as she entered. "He wants you to go to the police station right away."

Ignoring her yearning for a sandwich, Jenny turned

around and started walking to the police station.

"What is it?" she asked, bursting into Adam's room.

"We rounded up all the transients we found in the area. I think we might have found the man with the cart."

"Can you take me to him?"

"Would you be able to recognize him?"

"I haven't actually seen him," Jenny reminded Adam. "I saw him on tape just like you did."

Adam took her to a big one-way mirror and pointed to a bunch of men standing on the other side.

"They can't see you. Take your time, Jenny."

Jenny's gaze picked out the man right away.

"That's him," she said, pointing. "The man in that faded black shirt."

Adam spoke to one of his deputies. The men filed out one by one until the man Jenny had picked remained.

"Let's go in," Adam said.

Adam talked to the man. He seemed skittish and wouldn't answer any questions.

"We are not here to hurt you," Jenny spoke kindly. "We just need your help."

The man looked up and stared at her.

"We saw you at the gas station at the edge of town a few days ago. You were pushing a shopping cart."

The man shrugged.

"Do you remember that?"

"I walk around a lot," he finally said. "Lost track."

"There was a jacket in your shopping cart. The kid from the gas station took it from you."

The man grew disturbed. He talked about how he had been cold for a while.

"Where did you get that jacket?" Adam asked sternly. "Did you steal it?"

The man cowered, clamming up again. No amount of cajoling would make him speak. Adam threatened to arrest him.

Jenny stood up and went out. Adam followed her reluctantly.

"He's scared out of his wits," Jenny glared, her hands on her hips. "Can't you see that?"

"You need a firm hand with these people, Jenny," Adam growled. "Don't tell me how to do my job."

Ten futile minutes later, Adam came out again.

"We'll have to let him go. We have nothing to hold him here."

Jenny stood outside the police station, waiting for the man to come out. She saw him shuffle out of a side door.

"Hello," she called, walking up to him. "Can we talk a bit?"

"I didn't do anything," he said.

"I know that," Jenny said. "I'm not going to hurt you."

The man stared at her uncertainly.

"Let's walk away from here," Jenny suggested.

She led him out of sight of the station.

"My name is Jenny." She held out her hand.

The man hesitated. Then he grasped her hand in a tight grip and shook it.

"I run the café over yonder," Jenny told him. "The Boardwalk Café? I can get you something to eat."

"I don't know," the man said.

"My friend died here on this beach," Jenny said. "She was sitting on a bench over there and someone shot her."

The man's eyes filled with terror.

"Do you know anything about it?"

The man inched a few steps away from her.

"I know you didn't do anything. But I thought you might remember seeing someone. Anyone."

The man slowly shook his head.

"It's that jacket, you see?"

Jenny waited a few minutes for the man to say something. He was looking bewildered.

"Will you let me know if you remember anything? Come to the café when you are hungry. I mean it. I'll fix you up."

"Can I go now?" the man trembled.

Jenny nodded, trying to hide her disappointment. She was sure the man held some information which would be valuable to them. But she had no idea if she would ever see him again.

Back at the café, Star took one look at Jenny and ordered her to sit down. She placed a bowl of chicken soup before her, along with a turkey and cheddar sandwich.

"I'm taking an executive decision. We need a spa night."

Jenny wasn't sure she deserved to let her hair down but she went with the flow.

Heather and Betty Sue arrived at Seaview with Tootsie. Heather was carrying a basket in her arms.

"I have samples from local spas," she said. "I'm trying them out for the inn."

Heather had a bunch of new ideas to drum up business for the Bayview Inn. One of them involved a DIY spa weekend where groups of friends could hang out, giving each other makeovers.

Jenny picked up a lavender sugar scrub. Another small pot was labeled coffee mask.

"These look interesting, Heather."

"Why would someone spend money to stay at the inn?" Betty Sue grumbled. "Wouldn't they spend it at the spa?"

"We are giving them a homely atmosphere where they

can unwind with their friends," Heather explained. "The spa doesn't give them that. Many women are intimidated by the sterile environment."

"I agree with Heather," Jenny said, backing up her friend.

Molly arrived, holding a brown paper bag full of avocadoes.

"We are making my special avocado honey mask," she told them. "What are we eating?"

"Calzones from Mama Rosa's," Jenny told her. "And I'm hoping you will make your special brownie sundaes."

Molly pulled out a Tupperware container full of brownies from her bag.

Inevitably, the talk turned to Jenny's investigation.

Betty Sue spoke up. "The one question I can't answer is why Petunia. She never talked back to a seagull. Why kill her, that too in such a heinous manner?"

"It must be connected to her past," Star said. "She led a blameless life since she came to Pelican Cove."

"Are you saying she wasn't blameless when she lived back in Jersey?" Jenny asked.

"We don't know what kind of a person she was," Molly said. "She might have ruffled a few feathers. Or her husband did."

"Or her father?" Star asked darkly.

"So you are all sure Petunia's death has something to do with her mob family?" Jenny asked, looking around at each of them.

"That's the only logical explanation, Jenny," Heather said. "We don't have any other motive."

"So she always had a mark on her head?" Jenny asked them. "She just managed to evade it for twenty five years."

Chapter 18

Jenny parked her car outside the Boardwalk Café the next morning. Although the fall weather had produced some chilly mornings, it was a pleasant enough walk. But Jenny had taken to driving in since Petunia's accident.

The spa night had been good for all of them. The ladies had decided to sleep over at Seaview. They had given each other facials and watched movies until past midnight. Betty Sue and Heather had taken advantage of no guests at the inn. They were enjoying a rare opportunity to sleep in.

Jenny had promised them a grand breakfast at the café.

Jenny spied a figure sleeping against the café wall, huddled under a torn blanket. A shopping cart stood at one side, stuffed with trash bags. A gallon of water was tucked in between the bags. A faded camp chair was placed on top. A small one-eyed teddy bear sat on the folding shelf, giving Jenny a doleful stare.

Jenny didn't have the heart to wake up the man. She went in and started her daily routine. Soon, the café was filled with the aroma of fresh brewed coffee and muffins baking in the oven.

Jenny chopped onions and peppers and started beating

eggs for omelets. Captain Charlie, her favorite customer, came in and rang the tiny bell on the counter.

"Good Morning," Jenny greeted him. "Is it six already?"

"Dreaming about that young man of yours?" Captain Charlie teased.

Jenny had in fact been thinking of Petunia. She shook her head and placed a tall cup of coffee on the table.

"Muffins are coming right out."

Captain Charlie commented on the man sleeping outside.

"Seeing a lot of homeless men in town this year," he said.

"Where do they come from?"

"Anywhere, I guess. They are just down on their luck, looking for a square meal and a place to rest their head."

"Do you think they are violent?" Jenny asked.

"Very few of them are," Captain Charlie told her. "Some of them come from good backgrounds. They weren't always hobos."

Jenny thought about Captain Charlie's words long after he left. The breakfast rush had her scurrying around. The Magnolias came in around 8 AM.

"Crab omelets all around," Heather said, peeping into the kitchen. "Need some help?"

"I got this."

"Did you know there's a scary looking man sitting outside the café?"

"Are you talking about the man with the shopping cart?" Jenny asked. "Is he awake?"

"He's sitting up," Heather nodded. "Staring at the ground."

Jenny decided to check on the man after she served the Magnolias. She crossed her fingers and hoped it was the man from the gas station.

Twenty minutes later, she was standing outside the café, looking around for the man. The shopping cart lay against the wall. A neatly folded blanket lay on top of the trash bags. But the man was nowhere to be seen. Jenny looked around, beginning to feel frustrated. She didn't want to miss the opportunity to talk to the man. She walked around the café to the beach on a hunch. The man sat in the sand in a camp chair, staring out at the sea.

"Hello," Jenny called out.

He looked up and gave her a gap toothed smile.

"How about some coffee?"

The man shrugged and stared at her feet.

"Do you want to come inside?"

He stood up and folded his chair. He followed Jenny, carrying the chair in one hand. He put it in his cart when they reached the front.

"Do you like crab?" Jenny asked him. "I am making crab omelets."

The man shrugged again.

Jenny had spoken to the man the previous day so she knew he could talk. She guessed he was a man of few words.

Jenny showed him to a table near the window. He seemed comfortable in the café. She brought out a big platter, loaded with a three egg omelet, toast, juice and a flask of coffee.

"I'll be around if you need anything," Jenny told him.

She watched him from the kitchen. He took his time buttering his toast. Then he picked up his knife and fork and ate his omelet in small bites. Someone had definitely taught him the right table manners. Jenny remembered Captain Charlie's words. Her homeless guy must have come from a good life.

"More coffee?" Jenny asked him when he had eaten everything on his plate.

"Thanks," the man finally spoke.

"Did you like the food?" Jenny asked earnestly.

"Best I have eaten in a while," the man conceded. "Are you a trained chef?"

"Trained in the school of life," Jenny smiled.

"I thought about where I got the jacket," the man said. "It was somewhere around here, on this beach."

Jenny tried to curb her excitement.

"Was it lying somewhere?"

The man looked thoughtful.

"I don't think so. A man gave it to me."

He pointed a finger to his forehead.

"Memory's not what it used to be. It all runs together."

"Take your time," Jenny encouraged him. "There's no

rush."

"I was sitting on the beach in my chair. This man was walking around. He hung out here a lot, just like me."

"Do you remember what day it was?" Jenny asked.

"A few days ago," the man said. "Don't remember the exact day."

"Can you describe the man?" Jenny asked.

She wanted to ask if he was a hobo too. The man must have guessed what she was thinking.

"He was scruffy," he said thoughtfully. "But I don't think he slept on the beach, know what I mean?"

"That's a big help," Jenny said, thanking the man. "Did he say why he gave you the jacket?"

"Didn't ask," the man muttered. "Kind of threw it away without a backward glance. It was a perfectly good jacket."

The man stood up to leave. Jenny told him he was welcome at the café anytime. She packed a few muffins in a brown paper bag and handed it to the man.

"Thank you for your help."

"Good luck," the man nodded and left.

Jenny stood at the café door, waving goodbye as he pushed his cart down the street.

Jason Stone came up the street and hailed Jenny.

"Got any breakfast left? I'm starving."

"You won't believe who that was!" Jenny beamed with excitement as she set a loaded plate before Jason.

"Why did the guy throw away the jacket?" Jason asked, raising his eyebrows.

"He wanted to get rid of it, of course!"

"We can agree it was deliberate."

"It also means this wasn't an accident," Jenny said. "The guy ditched the jacket to avoid suspicion."

Jason cut off a big bite of omelet and wolfed it down.

"We always come back to the same point, Jenny. It was a man on this beach. Now who do we know who was definitely going to be here?"

"This homeless guy said the man was scruffy. He wasn't exactly a hobo but he wasn't normal either."

"Do you know anyone who fits that description?" Jason quizzed.

Jenny sat down before him, glad to rest her feet.

"You know what? I do!"

Jenny thought of the man who used to walk up and down the beach.

"There was a man here," she told Jason eagerly. "I spoke to him once or twice. He used to walk around here all the time, writing something in the sand."

"Writing what?"

"I don't know," Jenny said. "He used to scribble something with a stick and wait for the waves to wash it off."

Jason rolled his eyes.

"Where is this man now?"

"Haven't seen him in a while," Jenny said thoughtfully.

"Did he talk to anyone other than you?"

Jenny didn't have an answer for that. They talked about how they could look for the man. Jenny decided to talk to some of the beach regulars, like the woman who walked her dog every day.

Barb Norton came in, followed by a small mousy woman. She commandeered the biggest table in the café and sat down, setting a big pile of files down with a thud.

"I'm putting you down for five dozen chocolate cupcakes," Barb began, pointing a finger at Jenny. "And five dozen each of oatmeal raisin and lemon cookies."

"What are you talking about, Barb?" Jenny asked, bewildered.

"The bake sale?" Barb reminded her. "The Extermination Committee is holding one day after tomorrow. You would have known that if you had come to the last town meeting."

"But that's impossible," Jenny cried. "I told you I can't bake more than two dozen cookies."

"You have plenty of people to help you," Barb scowled, staring suggestively at Jason.

"I'm getting out of here," Jason mumbled.

"Sit down!" Barb ordered. "I'm not done with you."

"I'm no baker," Jason protested.

"Spread the word," Barb ordered. "Call clients up and down the coast. Get them here for the bake sale."

"Is that really going to help, Barb?" Jason asked. "How much money can you possibly raise selling cookies and cakes?"

Barb pulled out a sheet of paper from her file. Jason's eyes widened when he read what was on it.

"You can't possibly …"

"Leave that to me," Barb snapped. "You just focus on getting people here."

"Jason will do that," Jenny said, "but I can't contribute any more this time, Barb. I am already pushing the envelope here."

"You are one of us now, Jenny," Barb wheedled. "Don't you want to do your bit for the town?"

"The Boardwalk Café has always done its bit for the town," Jenny said firmly. "But I am sitting this one out. I have more important things to do."

"You're just blowing me off, girl. I won't forget this."

"Why are you harassing them, Barb?" Betty Sue Morse boomed. "Still yapping about those mosquitoes?"

"Someone has to do right by this town," Barb said pompously.

"You just manage to get everyone riled up," Betty Sue said.

The older women argued over past events where Barb had thrown her weight around. Jason crept out silently.

Jenny went into the kitchen, clutching her head.

"Are they still at it?" Heather asked gleefully.

She was chopping celery for the chicken salad.

The lunch crowd began trickling in as soon as Barb left. Jenny thought the day would never end. She forgot all about the man on the beach until dinner that night.

They had a simple meal of grilled fish and salad. It was a cool evening so they chose to sit in the cavernous family room at Seaview. Jenny closed her eyes and let herself be lulled by the sound of the ocean.

"We need to plan Petunia's memorial," Star reminded her. "At least finish planning the menu."

"I want to make all her favorites," Jenny said. "Vinny told me she liked those tiny cocktail meatballs."

Star looked surprised.

"I never knew that. She went along with pretty much everything."

They talked about Petunia for some time. Jenny's heart was heavy. She forced herself to go out for her walk.

She ran into Adam and Tank a few minutes later. Tank put his paws on her chest and licked her face.

"Get down, Tank," Jenny laughed. "Get down."

Adam smiled at her. Unlike Jason, Adam wasn't into impromptu hugs. Jenny was getting used to his standoffish nature.

"You remember that foliage trip we talked about last year?"

"We never made it," Jenny said.

"Why don't we go this weekend?" Adam asked eagerly. "I checked the foliage cam. The leaves are in peak color. It will be a beautiful drive."

"Are you serious?" Jenny asked.

"Of course. Skyline Drive is really beautiful this time of the year. We'll have a good time, Jenny."

"How can you be so insensitive, Adam?" Jenny glowered. "I haven't even buried my friend yet. Her killer is roaming around scot free."

"But ..."

Adam bit his lip and looked away.

"No matter what I do, I can't seem to please you, Jenny."

"I appreciate the thought, Adam," Jenny said,

swallowing a lump. "It's just not a good time for me right now."

"You mean it's not a good time for us!"

Chapter 19

It was a windy day at the beach. A middle aged man helped his two toddlers build a sand castle. A young couple waded into the ocean waves, hand in hand. Out on the deck of the Boardwalk Café, the Magnolias sampled the cinnamon apple muffins Jenny had baked that morning. She was trying out a new recipe for autumn.

"How's that Hopkins boy treating you?" Betty Sue asked Jenny.

Jenny had spent another sleepless night, agonizing over what she had said to Adam.

"He wants us to go away for the weekend," Jenny told the Magnolias.

The frothy waves of a high tide crashed against the shore. The Magnolias were enjoying their second cup of coffee.

"That sounds romantic," Heather sighed.

"It's callous, that's what it is," Jenny bristled. "I told him that."

Star and Betty Sue shared a look.

"You have to get on with your life, Jenny," Star said gently. "We all do."

Molly took Jenny's side.

"We all grieve at our own pace. I think Jenny's right."

"You might be pushing him away," Star warned. "He's already miffed because you didn't move in with him."

"I finally have a place I can call my own," Jenny said.

She had been a model wife for twenty years. Her husband had kicked her out one fine day. Jenny had vowed she would never give another man the opportunity to treat her like that again. When her divorce settlement came through, the first thing she had bought herself was a house. She intended to grow old in it, with or without a companion.

"You said it yourself, Star. We have to plan Petunia's memorial."

"We are all going to pitch in for that," Heather said. "If you want to spend a romantic weekend in the mountains, we will understand."

"Time and tide wait for no one," Betty Sue said heavily. "Petunia would want you to be happy, Jenny."

Jenny felt hemmed in from all sides.

"I'll think about it," she sighed.

Later, Jenny closed the café for the day and walked to Jason's office. She had remembered something and she needed his advice.

"Howdy Partner!" Jason greeted her.

"Am I disturbing you?"

"Not at all. I just finished up some paperwork. I do have court tomorrow, though."

"That man I was talking about yesterday," Jenny burst out. "He's the one who pulled that gun."

"Gun? How do I not know this?"

"This guy was arguing with someone for a long time and he suddenly pulled a gun out of his pocket. He ran off before anyone could report it."

"Who was he fighting with?"

Jenny's hands flew to her mouth.

"How could I forget that? It was Peter Wilson."

"The auto shop guy?"

"Yes! The guy Petunia was supposed to meet on the beach that fateful day."

"How is he connected to the man with the gun?"

"I don't know."

"But surely he knows the guy if he was fighting with him?"

"Let's find out."

Jenny didn't know where Peter Wilson lived. Jason told her that wasn't a problem.

"He must be at his shop. Let's go over there right now."

Jason pulled out his car and they reached Wilson's Auto Shop a few minutes later.

Peter Wilson recognized Jenny. He came over to greet them.

"Any new leads?" he asked hopefully.

"Not really," Jenny said. "But I have a few questions for you."

Peter smiled encouragingly.

"Remember the guy on the beach who pulled a gun on you?"

"Mason?"

Jenny turned toward Jason and groaned.

"That's right. I completely forgot his name was Mason."

"What do you want with him?" Peter Wilson asked.

"How is it that you know him?" Jenny asked. "Does he work for you?"

"No, he doesn't," Peter said. "He doesn't have a job as far as I know."

"Is he new in town?" Jason asked.

"Came here a few months ago," Peter nodded. "The Newburys hired him. But they let him go."

"Why?"

Peter Wilson shrugged.

"No idea. He wasn't a big talker."

"What were you fighting about that day?" Jenny asked curiously.

"I offered him a job," Peter explained. "Nothing big, just washing and detailing cars that come in here. He turned it down."

"That was nice of you," Jenny said. "Why did he pull a gun on you?"

"Said it was beneath him," Peter Wilson shrugged. "Accused me of working for his wife."

"Wife?"

"I'm as clueless as you are. Maybe the Newburys can tell you more."

Jenny and Jason thanked the mechanic and went back to their car.

"The Newburys are everywhere!" Jenny exclaimed. "They really do have a finger in every pie, don't they?"

"We'll have to go talk to them," Jason said. "Do you want to call ahead?"

The Newburys were the richest family in Pelican Cove. Rumor had it their riches came from sunken treasure. Ada Newbury considered herself a notch above the people in town. She didn't lose any opportunity driving it home.

"Ada will probably be too busy for us. I have an idea though."

Jenny asked Jason to make a pit stop at the Bayview Inn. She needed Betty Sue's help. Betty Sue and Ada were staunch rivals. Betty Sue's ancestor had been the original owner of the island. It had been called Morse Isle then. In addition to her impeccable heritage, Betty Sue was married to John Newbury, the head of the

Newbury family. Although long separated, Jenny knew the couple held each other in high regard.

"You are saying Ada knows this man with the gun?" Betty Sue asked.

"He's connected to the Newburys," Jenny explained. "We want to find out more."

Betty Sue called John Newbury and made sure he would be on hand to meet Jenny.

Jason drove up a hill toward the Newbury estate. Jenny watched the red, yellow and russet leaves on the trees and thought of Adam. She was sure she had done the right thing, refusing to go on the foliage trip.

"Penny for your thoughts," Jason said, his face stretched in a smile.

Jenny noticed the deeply etched laugh lines in Jason's face and the crinkles around his eyes. Jason's emotions were clearly written on his face. He seemed to be recovering well from his breakup. Jenny was glad to see shades of her old friend in that smile.

"Just enjoying the view," Jenny blushed.

"Me too, Jenny, me too," Jason winked.

Jason pulled up before a pair of massive iron gates. The guard in the small cabin spoke to someone with a walkie talkie and waved them through.

Jenny recognized the old housekeeper who let them in. She showed them into a cozy sitting room.

John Newbury stood up to greet them. He was a spry old man in his eighties, with a shock of thick white hair. Jason knew him well.

Ada Newbury sat stiffly in a wingback chair. She gave Jenny a slight nod.

A maid brought in a tea service. Jenny offered to pour the tea. Jason picked up a tiny cucumber sandwich and popped it in his mouth. John Newbury made some small talk. Ada glanced at her watch a couple of times.

"Feel free to leave any time, Ada," John said. "We don't want to hold you up."

Ada's nostrils flared but she said nothing.

John waited until Jenny took a few sips of her tea.

"What brings you here, dear?" he asked. "Betty Sue said it was urgent."

"Thank you for seeing us at such short notice," Jenny began.

Jason picked up a shortbread cookie from a tray and nodded.

"Do you know a man called Mason?"

"Mason Bush?" John asked. "We hired him as chief of security a while ago. But we had to let him go."

"May I ask why?"

John set his cup down and sighed.

"We hired him for the dispensary project. But it never materialized."

The Newburys had proposed setting up a medical marijuana farm and dispensary in Pelican Cove a few weeks ago. The town had strongly protested the idea. The outcry against the whole project had been so effective that the Newburys had failed to get the required licenses from the government. The project was scuttled before it got started.

"I am sorry about that," Jenny said sincerely. "I think it might have helped some people."

John shrugged.

"It wouldn't have worked without the town's approval."

"What happened to this guy after you fired him?" Jason asked.

"He was a good worker," John said. "Was in the

military, you know. We offered a generous pay package and a house to live in. He moved his family here from somewhere in the mid-west."

"So he wasn't local," Jenny murmured.

"He was excited about living in a beach town," John said. "His life went downhill after we let him go. His wife left him and filed for divorce. She wouldn't let him talk to the kids."

"But it wasn't his fault he lost the job?" Jenny asked.

"That's right," John said. "But the wife blamed him."

Jenny told him about the man she had seen wandering on the beach.

"I had no idea things were that bad!" John exclaimed. "We gave him a good severance package. I even offered to act as a reference."

"Would you say he was violent?"

John hesitated.

"Honestly, I never interacted with him much. My staff shortlisted him and interviewed him. I just saw him a couple of times when we had those meetings in town."

Ada spoke up.

"He escorted me a couple of times. He was quite jolly. He talked about his wife and kids all the time. Showed me a photo he carried in his wallet. But he changed overnight."

"How do you know that?" Jenny asked.

"I saw him walking around in town after we let him go," Ada told them. "He was unshaven. His clothes were streaked with mud. And I think he was drunk. He was swaying on his feet, muttering to himself."

"Did you talk to him?"

"I don't talk to riff-raff," Ada dismissed.

"Why are you asking so many questions about this man?" John wanted to know.

"He pulled a gun on someone down at the beach one day," Jenny explained. "He might be violent."

John Newbury couldn't hide his shock.

"I'm going to notify security about him immediately. Thanks for bringing this to my attention."

Jenny and Jason said goodbye.

"That was helpful!" Jenny complained as she settled in the car.

"Look on the bright side," Jason soothed. "We know the man's name. Adam can take it from here."

"Didn't Ada say the man was drunk?" Jenny asked a few minutes later. "Do you think he might have gone to the Rusty Anchor?"

Eddie Cotton, the proprietor of the Rusty Anchor, was quite good at remembering people. If Mason Bush had ever been to the pub, Eddie would know.

Jason drove to the Rusty Anchor, Jenny clinging on to the slight ray of hope she felt.

Her phone rang. It was John Newbury.

"Did I leave something behind?" Jenny asked.

"I remembered something," John said. "I called the office to double check before calling you."

"What is it?" Jenny asked, trying to curb her impatience.

"We provided a house for Mason Bush. He moved into it with his family. According to our severance package – I told you it was generous – he can stay there for two months after being let go."

"What does that mean, Mr. Newbury?"

"He's still living in that house," John said. "I made

sure he hasn't turned in the keys."

"Do you have the address?" Jenny asked with bated breath.

She motioned Jason to pull the car over.

"Can you write this down?"

"Give me a second," Jenny breathed, pulling an envelope out of her hand bag. She fished around for a pen. "Okay, tell me."

Jenny wrote the address John Newbury provided. She thanked him before hanging up.

She waved the envelope before Jason, her eyes shining with excitement.

"I know where he lives!"

Chapter 20

"Why don't you tell Adam about this?" Jason asked as he fed the address in the GPS.

"Let's go see if he's really living there," Jenny said.

Jason started driving and headed toward a set of houses by the water.

"This place seems familiar," Jenny said. "Have we been here before?"

Jason frowned and tried to think.

"Remember when we were tracing that car's route? One road led out of town. The other one led to a group of houses near the water."

Jenny nodded.

"This is where it led? I think we are getting warmer."

The address turned out to be a ranch style bungalow with a small dock at the back. A speedboat was tied to the dock. Jason parked in front of the house and they got out. The fading evening light cast long shadows as they stared at the house.

"Why don't you stay behind me, Jenny?"

"Don't be ridiculous!" Jenny exclaimed.

A car backfired just then and Jenny felt something whiz past her ear.

"Get down, Jenny," Jason cried. "He's shooting at us."

They ducked behind Jason's car. A couple more shots rang out.

"Do you think it's time to call Adam now?" Jason asked.

Jenny was already dialing her phone.

An engine sputtered to life just then. Jenny peeped from behind the car to see the boat speed away from the shore, leaving a frothy wake.

"He's getting away!" she cried, jumping up. "Do something, Jason!"

"What can I do?" Jason shrugged. "I don't see another boat here."

The speed boat was a mere speck by then.

"Jenny!" a voice crackled through Jenny's phone. "Hello, Jenny! Are you there?"

Jenny plastered her cell phone to her ear.

"He got away, Adam. Where are you? You need to get

here soon."

Adam rattled off a string of questions. Jenny calmed down enough to explain that Mason Bush had escaped using a boat.

"I'll be there in five minutes!" Adam said before hanging up.

Jenny leaned against Jason's car, frustrated.

"I'm sure they will catch him," Jason consoled her.

"But is he our man?" Jenny wanted to know.

"He shot at us," Jason said. "He also fled the scene. So he must be guilty of something."

"Do you think he's just crazy?"

"Be patient, Jenny," Jason reasoned. "We'll find out soon enough."

A police cruiser arrived in a cloud of dust and screeched to a stop. Adam hobbled out, leaning on his cane.

"I called the Coast Guard," he told them. "They have patrol boats out on the water. Now tell me everything from the beginning."

Jenny began with what the man with the shopping cart

had told her.

"You sat on this all this time?" Adam fumed.

"I told you about the man with the gun," Jenny said. "But you never brought him in."

Jason stepped in.

"Stop fighting, you two. What do we do next?"

"We wait," Adam said. "Why don't you two go home now?"

Jenny realized Adam was right.

Two days later, the Magnolias gathered at the Boardwalk Café, eager for the latest update.

Jenny brought out a plate of fresh blueberry muffins. Star was right behind her with a pot of coffee.

Betty Sue barely glanced at the food.

"So? Was it him? Tell us what you know."

Jenny sat down and poured herself a cup. She gave her friends a watery smile.

"Mason Bush confessed last night. He fired the shot that killed Petunia."

"Why?" Betty Sue cried. "What did she ever do to

him?"

Jenny felt the weight of her pent up emotions.

"It was a mistake."

The Magnolias started speaking at once. Jenny felt their outrage. She had been battling the same feelings since the previous night.

"What do you mean, Jenny?" Heather's question filtered through. "Was he just shooting his gun off on the beach?"

"He wanted to kill someone," Jenny said, stressing the last word. "It wasn't Petunia though."

"I'm guessing there is more to this story," Star said. "Start at the beginning, Jenny."

"Mason Bush was a decorated soldier," Jenny started. "He retired from the army and started looking for a job. He got one worthy of his qualifications."

"Is that when the Newburys hired him?" Molly asked.

Jenny nodded.

"The dispensary project was going to be big. Mason was hired as security chief. He had a bunch of people reporting to him. Unfortunately, the project fell through. The Newburys didn't have any need for him so they had to terminate his employment."

"Didn't he look for another job?" Heather asked.

"He must have. But he had a streak of bad luck. His wife left him. She took the kids. What's more, she refused to let him meet them."

"All because he lost that job?" Betty Sue asked.

"That part is not clear," Jenny shrugged. "Maybe they had some other differences. But Mason hit an all time low."

"Is that when he started roaming around like a homeless guy?" Molly queried.

"He was never homeless, really. He had a severance package and a house to live in. He probably had a pension too. He was just depressed."

"What does that have to do with our Petunia?" Star glowered.

"I'm coming to that. Mason started playing the blame game. He figured the town was responsible for him losing his job. And then he remembered the person who was at the forefront in all those protests."

"Who?" All voices yelled together.

"The person who made sure the Newburys didn't get

the necessary licenses for their project. The person who saw to it that the project got scuttled."

"Barb Norton," Betty Sue said under her breath.

"Barb Norton?" Molly and Heather cried.

Jenny gave a deep sigh.

"Mason wanted revenge. He decided the only way he would get it was by killing Barb."

"What happened on the beach that day?" Star asked.

Jenny paused to recollect what Adam had told her.

"Mason couldn't sleep. He was walking on the beach when he saw Petunia sitting on that bench. She was the same height and build as Barb. And she was wearing a scarf that looked a lot like something Barb has."

"He thought she was Barb," Star said, welling up.

Jenny nodded.

"He pulled out his gun and shot her. He said he didn't give it much thought."

"He must have fled the scene though, huh?" Heather asked. "He didn't come forward when the police were making their inquiries."

"I guess his survival instincts kicked in when he

realized what he had done. He drove his car out of the parking lot. He had done a survey of the town's security systems. He knew about the traffic cameras. He parked his car in the woods and just walked home. He retrieved his car later."

"What about that jacket?" Molly asked. "Wasn't that what led you to him?"

"Mason realized the jacket might put him on the spot. He handed it over to a man on the beach."

There was a stunned silence as the Magnolias digested the story.

"It's not fair!" Molly wailed indignantly. "So Petunia's only fault was she was in the wrong place at the wrong time."

"We have to send her off in style," Betty Sue said in a heavy voice, dabbing her eyes with a lace handkerchief. "Pretty much all we can do now."

Jenny and the ladies banded together to fulfill Petunia's last wishes. She was cremated and her ashes were scattered at sea, the girls saying their final goodbye as they stood on the deck of Captain Charlie's boat.

Jason covered Jenny with his jacket and held her as she cried her eyes out.

Petunia had approved a memorial. The Magnolias got

busy planning a grand party. The whole town was invited. Jenny made all her signature dishes, ones Petunia had loved. There were crab puffs, and pimento cheese, chocolate cupcakes and strawberry cheesecake. Jenny made tiny meatballs using a recipe she found in Petunia's diaries.

The Boardwalk Café wore a festive air the day of the memorial. Any tourist might have mistaken it for a happy occasion. But the moist eyes and bittersweet expressions on the women's faces told a different story.

Adam stood close to Jenny with a protective arm around her shoulders.

"Let's get away somewhere," Jenny said.

"You mean now?" Adam asked.

"Not now. Tomorrow. Later. I'm beginning to suffocate here, Adam. I want some time away from here."

"Okay," Adam agreed. "Where do you want to go?"

"Enough with the questions," Jenny snapped, leaving Adam bewildered.

Heather pulled Jenny aside and hissed in her ear.

"What is she doing here?"

Barb Norton had arrived, wearing her usual pompous expression.

"She's got some gall, coming here," Star bristled, coming to stand beside Jenny.

Mason Bush had confessed to attacking Barb in the street. The police told her how he mistook Petunia for her and shot her. Barb hadn't been seen around town after that. Everyone hoped she would go visit her daughter in Florida for a few days.

"I'm asking her to leave," Heather seethed.

Betty Sue had sidled up to them.

"It's not her fault," she sighed. "Let her pay her respects."

Barb walked up and opened her arms. She hugged each of them.

"I am so sorry," she said sincerely. "I know that doesn't change anything. I am going to miss Petunia."

"It's not your fault," Betty Sue said again. "Thank you for coming here, Barb."

Jenny gritted her teeth and spoke about the weather.

A screech of tires sounded outside. A stream of big, black SUVs with dark windows came to a stop outside the café. The Bellinis had arrived.

Vinny and his cohorts got out of one car. Vinny wore a dark suit and a dark fedora. Enzo Bellini stepped out of the second car, wearing a black track suit with his signature white hat. Charles and Laura stepped out of the third car. They made a grand entrance into the café.

Enzo pumped Jenny's hand and thanked her profusely.

"Thank you for catching my baby girl's killer."

Vinny had spotted the meatballs-on-a-stick. He popped one in his mouth and walked toward Jenny.

"Great party, sweetheart! Thanks for doing this."

"Thank you for coming," Jenny muttered, feeling overwhelmed.

She wondered why the Bellinis were still hanging around Pelican Cove. Vinny answered her unspoken question.

"Had to tie up some loose ends ... we are getting out of town after this party."

"Your mother would be glad you came," Jenny told him.

Vinny looked around the packed café.

"Our Ma had a good life here. Are you going to keep the café going?"

Jenny nodded.

"I love this place. You don't mind Petunia left it to me?"

"Not at all. You take care of this place for her."

He pulled out a card from his pocket and handed it to her.

"Call me if you need anything. We take care of our own."

He tipped his hat and wished her good luck. He walked out, flanked by his three men.

Jenny and her friends began tidying up the café. The party moved to Seaview, Jenny's seaside house.

Jason took drink orders from everyone. Adam sat next to Jenny, peering at her with concern.

"I'm not going to break, Adam," Jenny grumbled. "Relax!"

"I know it was a tough day," he said, rubbing Jenny's palm. "But you handled it well."

Heather raised her glass in a toast.

"To Petunia ... may she rest in peace."

Everyone raised their glasses and toasted their dear friend.

"To Petunia."

Star sat up suddenly.

"I almost forgot, Jenny."

She went inside and came out with a big sketchbook.

"These are just some designs I have been working on."

Jenny opened the book curiously, and gasped when she saw the drawing inside.

"You talked about sprucing up the café," Star explained. "I thought you might want a new logo."

Jenny stared at the lifelike caricature of Petunia juxtaposed next to some pretty lettering.

"I love it," Jenny squealed, handing the sketchbook to Heather.

Everyone wholeheartedly approved the new logo.

Adam's phone rang shrilly, making Jenny jump. He stood up and walked into the next room to take the call.

Jenny was the only one watching when he came back.

"What's the matter?" she asked, dreading his reply.

"That was the station," Adam said, dumbfounded. "Mason Bush is dead. He was found stabbed in his cell."

Epilogue

The car climbed into the mountains, following the serpentine road. Tall firs towered over them, ablaze in vivid tones of yellow and orange. There was a riot of color wherever Jenny looked.

"Skyline Drive stretches over a hundred miles in the Blue Ridge Mountains," Adam told her.

Jenny had finally caved and agreed to go on the foliage trip with Adam. She fought against the happiness bubbling inside her. Wasn't it wrong to feel such joy when she had just lost her close friend?

"You up for a small hike?" Adam asked, clutching her hand tighter and planting a feather light kiss on her forehead.

They had been holding hands since they left Pelican Cove. Adam had refused to let go. Jenny thought it was romantic. Her heart beat in anticipation of what was coming next.

Adam parked near a trail head and they got out. Adam packed some snacks and drinking water in a backpack and slung it over his shoulder.

"It's about three miles to the falls but they should be worth it," he told Jenny.

Jenny set a leisurely pace as they walked down the trail. They passed a few hikers on the way. They heard the falls before they saw them.

Adam helped Jenny onto a rocky ledge that provided a good view of the waterfall. Jenny looked down on the water, drinking in the beauty of the scene.

She heard a throat clear and whirled around instinctively. The sight before her took her breath away, more so than the churning water below.

Adam Hopkins was down on one knee, holding up a tiny box. He popped it open, making Jenny's eyes go wide and her mouth drop.

"Will you marry me, Jenny King?"

THE END

Thank you for reading this book. If you enjoyed this book, please consider leaving a brief review. Even a few words or a line or two will do.

As an indie author, I rely on reviews to spread the word about my book. Your assistance will be very helpful and greatly appreciated.

I would also really appreciate it if you tell your friends and family about the book. Word of mouth is an author's best friend, and it will be of immense help to me.

Many Thanks!

Author Leena Clover

http://leenaclover.com

Leenaclover@gmail.com

http://twitter.com/leenaclover

https://www.facebook.com/leenaclovercozymysterybooks

Other books by Leena Clover

Pelican Cove Cozy Mystery Series –

Strawberries and Strangers

Cupcakes and Celebrities

Berries and Birthdays

Sprinkles and Skeletons

Waffles and Weekends

Parfaits and Paramours

Meera Patel Cozy Mystery Series -

Gone with the Wings

A Pocket Full of Pie

For a Few Dumplings More

Back to the Fajitas

Christmas with the Franks

Acknowledgements

This book would not have been possible without the support of many people. I am thankful to my beta readers and advanced readers and all my loved ones who provide constant support and encouragement. A big thank you to my readers who take the time to write reviews or write to me with their comments – their feedback spurs me on to keep writing more books.

Join my Newsletter

Get access to exclusive bonus content, sneak peeks, giveaways and much more. Also get a chance to join my exclusive ARC group, the people who get first dibs on all my new books.

Sign up at the following link and join the fun.

Click here →
http://www.subscribepage.com/leenaclovernl

I love to hear from my readers, so please feel free to connect with me at any of the following places.

Website – http://leenaclover.com

Twitter – https://twitter.com/leenaclover

Facebook – http://facebook.com/leenaclovercozymysterybooks

Email – leenaclover@gmail.com

Made in the USA
Coppell, TX
30 August 2020

34818944R10156